THE SECRET DEAD CLUB

ALSO BY KAREN STRONG

Just South of Home

Eden's Everdark

THE SECRET DEAD CLUB

KAREN STRONG

Simon & Schuster Books for Young Readers
NEW YORK   LONDON   TORONTO   SYDNEY   NEW DELHI

SIMON & SCHUSTER BOOKS FOR YOUNG READERS
An imprint of Simon & Schuster Children's Publishing Division
1230 Avenue of the Americas, New York, New York 10020
This book is a work of fiction. Any references to historical events, real people, or real places are used fictitiously. Other names, characters, places, and events are products of the author's imagination, and any resemblance to actual events or places or persons, living or dead, is entirely coincidental.
Text © 2024 by Karen Strong
Jacket illustration © 2024 by Vivienne To
Jacket design by Lucy Ruth Cummins
All rights reserved, including the right of reproduction in whole or in part in any form.
SIMON & SCHUSTER BOOKS FOR YOUNG READERS
and related marks are trademarks of Simon & Schuster, LLC.
Simon & Schuster: Celebrating 100 Years of Publishing in 2024
For information about special discounts for bulk purchases, please contact Simon & Schuster Special Sales at 1-866-506-1949 or business@simonandschuster.com.
The Simon & Schuster Speakers Bureau can bring authors to your live event. For more information or to book an event, contact the Simon & Schuster Speakers Bureau at 1-866-248-3049 or visit our website at www.simonspeakers.com.
Interior design by Hilary Zarycky
The text for this book was set in New Caledonia.
Manufactured in the United States of America
0724 BVG
First Edition
2 4 6 8 10 9 7 5 3 1
Library of Congress Cataloging-in-Publication Data
Names: Strong, Karen, author.
Title: The Secret Dead Club / Karen Strong.
Description: First edition. | New York : Simon & Schuster Books for Young Readers, 2024.
Identifiers: LCCN 2023027921 (print) | LCCN 2023027922 (ebook) |
ISBN 9781665904506 (hardcover) | ISBN 9781665904520 (ebook)
Subjects: CYAC: Ability—Fiction. | Ghosts—Fiction. | Friendship—Fiction. | Clubs—Fiction. | Middle schools—Fiction. | Schools—Fiction. | LCGFT: Ghost fiction. | Novels.
Classification: LCC PZ7.1.S79642 Se 2024 (print) | LCC PZ7.1.S79642 (ebook) | DDC [E]—dc23
LC record available at https://lccn.loc.gov/2023027921
LC ebook record available at https://lccn.loc.gov/2023027922

*For secret clubs everywhere.
Love and protect your friends.*

PART ONE
A HAUNTED HOUSE

The Callahan House, November 7, 1946

On Noble Avenue, in the Queen Anne Victorian house his grandfather had built, Caleb Callahan shivered in his bed.

The frigid temperature had nothing to do with the time of year, and Caleb understood the reason why his teeth chattered. Burrowing his head deeper under the cocoon of blankets, he hid from the dead thing in his room.

At first, the sight of his mother's ghost ignited a yearning hope inside him. Death had restored her rosy cheeks and vibrant red hair. After Caleb's mother had died, a heavy despair had settled into the house. It sank into the floors, pressed against the windows, and covered the walls. For his sister and father, the deep sorrow crawled under their skin and disappeared into their bones. For Caleb himself, the bleak sadness hadn't yet pierced his heart.

Caleb knew the ghost wasn't his mother, but he didn't know the dead woman in his room had died long before his mother was born. She'd already claimed dozens of souls before Caleb's grandfather laid the first brick of his house in 1892. Cruel and full of trickery, this woman could easily shift into any of her stolen forms, and for tonight's purposes, she wore the face of the deceased Dorothea Callahan.

Strong hands tugged at Caleb's blankets. He fought to keep a grip on his hiding place, but he quickly lost the battle. Exposed to the frosty air, he squeezed his eyes shut.

"Don't be afraid, Caleb."

He let out a whimper at the sound of his mother's voice. It was the same soothing tone that had told him about the streetcars that once rolled down the wide avenue outside his window.

When the dead thing grabbed his shoulder, Caleb scrambled across the bed and fell hard to the floor. Blinking in the murky room, he let out a quivering breath and puffs of warm air drifted out of him like white smoke. Slowly, he peeked from the edge of the bed.

His mother stood on the other side. The lamppost outside his window lit up half her face while the other half remained in shadow. She wore the same black dress as the one from her coffin. A jeweled brooch on her collar glittered in the gloom. Caleb had given it to his mother as a birthday gift.

Doubt crept into Caleb's chest, but he held firm to his will. His mother would never try to hurt him. No matter what this dead thing wanted, he wouldn't fall for its tricks.

"You're a special boy, Caleb," the ghost whispered sweetly. "You don't have to fight me."

When the dead thing revealed teeth in a ghastly version of a smile, Caleb ducked behind the bed and squeezed his eyes shut again. The sound of footsteps made its way around to the side of his bed, and the bitter cold seeped through his pajamas and nipped at his skin.

"Don't make this difficult, Caleb." The woman was no longer being sweet, and her voice was full of hunger. "I promise to take good care of you. *All your life.*"

When her icy hands grabbed him again, Caleb screamed. A heavy pressure landed on his chest and he panted in agony at the tight squeezing of his heart. The dead thing's menacing thoughts swam in his head before it gave him a harsh command to surrender.

A gentle tug pulled at him as the angry voice faded and the pain in his chest stopped. Warm air caressed his face, and when he opened his eyes, Caleb was no longer in his grandfather's house.

Beyond his body, Caleb's soul had traveled to a nameless yet familiar place. He blinked as he surveyed an endless meadow of wildflowers. A golden sun hung in a perfect blue sky, and grass swayed around him in the gentle breeze.

When he was a smaller child, Caleb's mother had taken him here for picnics. He knew this meadow was different from the real one, yet it gave him the same emotions as being in a lucid dream. He turned to the horizon and squinted at a lone figure in the distance.

Moments after Caleb screamed, the bedroom door opened and his sister rushed into the room. Barbara Callahan found her brother trembling on the floor.

Above her, the woman crouched on the ceiling in her true form. Death revealed rotting flesh and tattered hair. A tunic, now black with decay, melded to her exposed rib cage. If Barbara had looked up, she might have fainted at the grisly sight, but unlike her brother, she couldn't see the dead.

Barbara pulled Caleb close and kissed his forehead. The room was cold, and Barbara gathered her robe around her neck.

"Wake up, Caleb."

When her brother didn't respond, she shook him until his eyes opened. Barbara gasped at the emptiness she saw in them. No spark of life churned in his hollow gaze. A bright panic rose inside her until an awareness bloomed on her brother's face. When he finally smiled at her, Barbara let out a jumble of relieved laughter.

Since her mother's death, she'd become the lady of the house, taking over all the responsibilities and worries. She had to care for not only her brother, but her father as well. Grief had robbed Samuel Callahan of sleep, and he'd taken up the habit of sitting at his desk in the library. Many nights Barbara would find her father staring into space, glassy-eyed and mournful. During these late hours, she would coax him back upstairs to his bed. Although her father's behavior lay heavy on her heart, she worried most about her little brother.

"Your bad dream has ended," Barbara said with a certainty she hoped sounded true. "Everything will be all right now."

Caleb watched the dead thing crawl down from the ceiling. He'd never seen the woman in her true form, and now it was too late to close his eyes.

Barbara sensed her brother's terror and slowly turned to look behind her, but she couldn't see the vicious glee on the worm-eaten, skeletal face. She couldn't see the woman leave the room.

A pounding alarm rang in Caleb's ears. Where was the dead thing going? Not knowing the answer sent a sharp bolt of horror up his spine.

Downstairs in the library, Samuel Callahan sat in the dark. His eyes pooled with unshed tears, until the heavy mourning released salty trails down his face. The strongest member of the Callahan family had become the weakest. He yearned to redeem his bedrock role for the sake of his children, but his wife's death tormented his mind and agonized his heart.

When he shuddered from an unknown chill, it meant nothing to him. Unlike his son, he couldn't see the woman showcasing his wife's stolen face, but he felt the frozen kiss on his lips. He didn't know the woman was giving him a rare grace; Samuel only shivered from the cold.

The woman had come to the house specifically for the boy, but now she found the father's suffering attractive. His pain would be useful. For both the living and the dead, sorrow dwelled very close to anger. The father's body held no gifts, but the woman itched for revenge. The woman had always claimed what she wanted, and the boy vexed her. She would punish him for his resistance.

When Samuel felt the odd intrusion in his body, he hitched his breath in surprise. A presence stirred in his chest like a serpent, and it coiled tight around his heart. The pressure increased until vengeful rage replaced deep sadness. When the darkness fell upon him, Samuel couldn't escape to the nameless place like his son had. The woman easily captured his soul. The numbness freed him from his pain, and he accepted the vicious lies that slithered around in his head.

Standing up from the desk, the woman left the library in her latest stolen form. She'd always preferred the living over the dead. She admired Samuel Callahan's large, strong hands as she slowly ascended the staircase.

Later, they would say it had been the father's inconsolable grief that drove him to commit the heinous crimes. Only true madness could be responsible for such shocking deaths. Others would say a curse had marked the Callahans. Only deep evil could take the lives of innocent children.

Many would speculate about the family's tragedy, but only Caleb held the truth of what happened that night. Although he no longer shivered in his bed, he still remained inside his grandfather's house.

CHAPTER ONE

Nana's house doesn't look haunted.

The pale yellow Victorian has a gable roof and lots of windows. Skinny white columns support a wraparound porch with decorative trim. There's even a circular tower topped with a weather vane that Olivia says we must call a turret out of respect.

I've seen plenty of photos of my great-grandmother's house online, and I'm familiar with its history. Olivia made sure to tell me what happened to the Callahan family when I was old enough to understand.

"Wednesday!" Olivia yells from the back of our car as she unloads the trunk. "I can't find the house key. Go let them know we're here."

I cross the sidewalk to the black wrought-iron fence surrounding the yard and open the gate. The yard has bare spots even though a brand-new water hose snakes through tall, dry weeds. The porch has a thick layer of dust on its wood-planked floors, and cobwebs fill the corners. I cover my nose to keep from sneezing. Before I can ring the doorbell, Jasmine opens the door and pulls me in for a hug.

"You made it!" Her excited voice vibrates against my chest.

When she lets me go, Lincoln has joined us on the porch, and he quickly squashes me into another hug. Jasmine runs down the steps to the curb, and Olivia shrieks in happiness.

"How was the drive?" Lincoln's dark brown skin radiates in the afternoon light. He and his partner, Jasmine, are Olivia's friends and my godparents. They don't live in Nana's house, but they've been taking care of it while we've been away.

"Smooth sailing," I tell him.

Lincoln is a familiar face from Olivia's video chats. In person, he smells like sugar like I knew he would. He inherited a bakery and still uses his family's recipes.

"Y'all have to forgive the yard." He ducks his head. "Jasmine has been teaching all summer, and I'm always at work. We don't come by here as often as we should."

"It doesn't look that bad," I say. "I'm sure Olivia won't mind."

Lincoln widens his eyes and lets out a booming laugh. "Don't think I'll get over you calling your mama by her first name."

Jasmine and Olivia join us on the porch with arms full of boxes. Both of them have huge grins on their faces. Best friends reunited.

"Liv, I see you haven't found your home training yet." Lincoln takes the boxes out of her hands. "Wednesday is still using your government name."

"For the record, she can call me Mama or whatever, but only if she wants."

My mother's right. She did give me a choice when I was a small kid, but calling her anything but Olivia feels wrong in my mouth. Maybe one day that will change.

"Nothing about this surprises me," Jasmine says. "But seriously, Liv. Your grandma wouldn't have liked it."

Olivia laughs. "I don't think she would have cared."

"Oh, she would have cared. I don't recall you ever calling your grandma *Josephine*." Lincoln winks at me before he walks into the house with Olivia's boxes.

I follow them inside to a small entry room. A green-tiled fireplace is on one side, and a painted wall with a coat rack is on the other. After admiring the leaded glass of the front door, I move deeper into the house. It has an interesting smell: old paper mixed with warm cooking spices. The crystal chandelier hanging above me looks like the original fixture. Unlike the yard and the porch, the interior of the house is spotless. Olivia looks around with satisfied approval.

"Not gonna lie, Liv. I've been so busy, and I knew the place would be a dusty wreck," Jasmine says. "So I called a cleaning service. They pulled the sheets off everything and performed a miracle."

We follow Jasmine and Lincoln and gather around the small kitchen island where a large fruit basket is wrapped in plastic and tied with a red ribbon.

"Y'all haven't had any problems, right?" Olivia asks. "Tell me the truth."

Jasmine gives Lincoln a quick look. "You mean with the

Callahan ghost? You think we would be coming to check on this place if he gave us any trouble?"

"We know Black folks don't do haunted houses, but it hasn't been a problem for us," Lincoln adds.

"Good." Olivia's face relaxes. "Nana promised nothing bad would happen here again."

Before my great-grandmother bought this house, it had remained mostly empty—no one would ever stay within its walls for long because the Callahan ghost would drive them away. But when Nana moved in, she gave respect to Caleb Callahan. Maybe this is why some of the rooms have their original fixtures and the house is still painted a pale yellow—an unspoken agreement between the living and the dead.

"Liv, you mentioned you had something important to share with us," Lincoln says. "What is it?"

Olivia fiddles with the ribbon on the fruit basket before she looks at me, and my stomach gurgles. I slowly nod to give her permission.

"It's partly true we decided to come back to Alton because it'll be good for Wednesday to enroll in school and be around people her age. We've been on the road for a while now, but I can do my art anywhere...." Olivia's voice trails off.

"What happened, Liv?" Jasmine carefully asks.

Olivia reaches for my hand and squeezes it. "Wednesday was using her gift to help a lost spirit like she usually does, but it turned out to be wicked."

Jasmine's eyes widen, and Lincoln stares at me with

concern. Olivia and I call ghosts by many common names, but only a wicked one can harm the living. They can change their appearance and mimic other ghosts. Most dangerous of all—they like to possess the living who have special talents, including those who can see the dead.

"Y'all know Nana was blessed with her gift all her life," Olivia continues. "My mama lost hers. Same with me. That's probably going to happen to Wednesday too, but I don't want to take any more chances on the road."

Jasmine and Lincoln know about our family's ability to communicate with ghosts. Olivia has told them about the different types, so they already know how dangerous the wicked ones can be. Olivia has warned me about wicked ghosts too, but I never thought I would ever encounter one.

"Where did this happen?" Lincoln's voice is low and quiet.

"Arizona. On a campground in the state park not far from Route 191," Olivia answers in a tight voice.

A lump in my throat rises as I try to push the memory away, but I'm swooshed back into the dark forest. A ghost of a lost child turning into something else. The hot wave of nausea. Olivia's frantic face. It was the only time I'd ever been truly terrified of the dead.

"Are you okay?" Lincoln asks me.

His voice pulls me back to the safety of the kitchen. My mouth feels stuffed with cotton, and I swallow. "Yeah, I'm fine."

"I got us as far away as possible," Olivia quickly adds.

"We drove back to Vegas, and that's when I started making plans to come here. Since then, we haven't had any problems."

"Does Desmond know about this?" Jasmine whispers.

"I've spoken with him, and he isn't too happy about it. As usual, he has plenty of opinions."

Hearing my father's name sends a rush of worry through me. He's never liked the idea of me and Olivia traveling alone and argued it was unsafe. We have video chats because he's in London completing his medical residency. My father is always happy to see me, despite the dark circles under his eyes from his long shifts. His British accent is much stronger now too. We don't talk about my gift at all. It's the topic I dodge with him because I know it makes him uncomfortable. My father has always been a man of pure science, and ghosts are something he's not willing to accept as real. Olivia could never convince him that our family gift was authentic.

Jasmine hugs me. "Wednesday, what an awful experience. I'm so glad you're okay."

Since that terrible night in the Arizona state park, I haven't seen any ghosts, but I know that will change living in Nana's house and in Alton, one of the oldest cities in Georgia.

Olivia has assured me that wicked ghosts are rare. She believes I should honor our family tradition, but I don't know which ghosts I can trust. I'm not sure if I can tell the difference between the ones who are harmless and the ones who want to hurt me, so I've decided not to help any ghosts at all.

I'm going to ignore the dead.

CHAPTER TWO

Olivia and I don't have much, since we lived in an RV for two years. We traveled the Southwest while Olivia created and sold her mixed-media art. We only carried what we needed. The RV was cozy, with a kitchen, small living area, and a queen bed that we shared during our adventures.

I explore the first floor of Nana's house, and the den is different from the other formal, stuffy rooms. There's a cozy sectional sofa with mismatched pillows, and a leather recliner sits in the corner. A thin rug rests under a table that's cluttered with dog-eared paperbacks and art books. I smile when I recognize some of the board games stacked on the floor near the fireplace.

"What do you think?" Olivia asks from the den's open sliding doors.

"There's a lot of stuff in this house," I say.

"That's what happens when you have a lot of space."

If Olivia had it her way, she would buy a tiny house and live off the grid. Despite the fact that Nana's house is haunted, Olivia has had many offers from eager real estate agents. But she promised my great-grandmother that she would never sell and would pass it down to me. One day, this house would be mine—ghost and all.

Olivia pushes my braids from my face. "You ready to see your room?"

I follow her up the staircase. Some steps creak louder than others—especially the one at the very top. When we reach the first landing, she points to a narrow set of stairs leading to the third level of the house.

"That's how you get to the turret. My old studio is still up there. Gets plenty of good light. I'm looking forward to working in it again."

On the second floor, two bedrooms face each other. Farther down the hall, there's a bathroom, another bedroom, and back stairs leading to the kitchen.

Olivia opens the door to her left to reveal a room with bare walls and hardwood floors. My suitcase rests on an iron platform bed. There's a nightstand, and a wood-framed mirror is attached to a chest of drawers. I walk to the bay window that faces the front yard. Parting the lace curtains, I spot our car parked on the curb. Outside the house across the street, a girl around my age sits on the front steps, her dark hair hiding her face.

"You can decide what else you want to put in here," Olivia tells me. "There's enough room for a desk and chair."

The room already smells like me: a mix of coconut oil and vanilla. I sit on the bed and examine my pink and lavender braids.

A few nights after my ghost ordeal in Arizona, Olivia

bought a bulk package of different color bundles at a beauty supply store in Las Vegas. Later inside the RV, she braided the different hues into my hair. The quiet sliding of Olivia's fingers and our synced breaths were the only sounds. Looking at the braids soothed me, and I started to believe I would be okay.

Olivia joins me on the bed, and her eyes look tired from the drive. We share the same heart-shaped face, dimples, and long, thick hair. Olivia keeps hers in locs, and I like to keep mine in braids. Her bronze skin is scattered with freckles while I have my father's brown tone, but we share the same smile.

I was born in Alton, but then we moved to Boston when I was a baby and my father got accepted to medical school. Growing up, I tried my best to blend in with the other kids, but I was afraid of them finding out about my gift. "I see dead people" isn't the kind of thing you can casually bring up in a conversation, and Boston had plenty of ghosts. Since I didn't want to be known as a freak, I convinced myself it was okay to be a loner—so no party invites, no sleepovers, no best friends.

When my parents broke up, Olivia gave me a choice: I could go to London and live with my father's family or remain with her and travel to the Southwest. It was an easy decision for me. I didn't want to start all over again in a new country. At least with Olivia homeschooling me in the RV, no one could reject me, and I wouldn't have to hide who I truly am. Everything was perfect—until the wicked ghost found me.

I look at the bare walls and clean floors, thinking of the horrible things that happened in this house.

"Whose room was this?" I ask.

Olivia blinks for a moment as if my question has surprised her. "This used to be my room, but before that it was Caleb's room. It's the second biggest one after Nana's room down the hall. I decided to take Barbara's old room so you could have this one."

When Olivia first told me about the Callahans, I searched for them online. A ghost with a tragic history is the easiest to find. In one photo of the family, Caleb Callahan is sitting next to his older sister, Barbara, and their father is standing behind them. By that time, their mother, Dorothea, had already died of pneumonia. Caleb and his sister are smiling, but their father, Samuel, looks grim. The photo is notorious because it was taken just a few weeks before the family's tragic end.

"Do you think I'll see Caleb?" I ask, trying to push down the rising alarm in my chest.

Olivia moves closer to me. "Does that worry you? Despite what people say, Caleb isn't dangerous."

Instead of answering her, I examine my braids again. I'm not sure if I'm ready to interact with ghosts yet—not when thinking about them makes my heart gallop in panic.

"We've been through a lot," Olivia says. "Do you want to talk about what happened with the wicked spirit?"

I want to tell her about the spiraling thoughts and how they churn in my brain like a storm. I want to tell her about the bad dreams and the vivid flashbacks. But I don't want her to worry about me, even though I know she already does.

"I've been really scared," I confess.

"Me too," Olivia admits. "I feel awful because it was my fault."

I frown. "No it wasn't."

"I was naive, Wednesday. After all those years in Boston when nothing bad happened to you, I assumed you would be safe everywhere. I was wrong, and I'm so sorry. If it hadn't been for your Lodestar . . ." Olivia kisses me and squeezes me tight. "I'm so happy I didn't lose you."

Lodestars are a form of protection—a guiding light we follow to protect our souls from possession. No one in our family knows how we inherited this self-defense or who was the first person to use this power. Olivia tells me the details have been lost through years of oral history. Every descendant has a dormant Lodestar inside them—activated in danger to guide our soul when it needs to flee our body and then to lead us back when it's safe to return.

Olivia never had to use her Lodestar, so she couldn't tell me where our souls go when we leave our bodies. When she asked me what happened with my Lodestar, I told her I only saw a blank void—a vast white nothingness.

The harrowing experience in Arizona still terrifies me. What if my Lodestar didn't work that night? What terrible things would have happened to me?

"Family traditions don't always have to be honored," Olivia whispers in my ear. "You don't have to speak with spirits anymore, Wednesday. Not if they make you feel unsafe."

She releases me from her hug, and tight knots unravel

in my stomach. "I'm not sure what I want to do right now."

Her eyes fill up with concern. "I would say take all the time you need, but I don't know how much time you have left."

Our family also doesn't know why we lose our ability to speak with the dead after we hit puberty. Only a rare few keep their gifts for their entire lifetimes. Nana was the first in our family in over a century. In June, I got my period while we were at Yosemite National Park, and Olivia made my favorite casserole to celebrate. I expected my gift to fade, but over the next few weeks, I didn't see any difference. Then the wicked ghost found me in Arizona.

"I know I'll probably lose my gift soon," I say softly.

"I took mine for granted until I lost it. . . ." Olivia stares at the comforter on the bed. "I don't want you to have any regrets when that happens."

I think about the ghosts I've encountered. The ones I befriended in Boston and helped cross over. The ghosts in Las Vegas with unfinished business. The others I met on the road at gas stations, rest stops, and diners—the desperate ones who needed a witness to listen or a connection to get information. Would I regret ignoring the dead who truly needed my help?

Without my gift, I would live a different existence. Ghosts would become a memory. But without my gift I would also get relief from the turmoil currently living in my body.

"When it happens, I'll be ready," I tell Olivia.

CHAPTER THREE

After we eat pizza for dinner, Olivia suggests I go explore Nana's room.

When I open the door, gold frames on the walls display relatives dressed in fancy suits and dresses. I stare at photos of Nana as a chubby baby, a young girl, and a beautiful woman.

My grandmother, Lucille, appears in framed photos on the wall too. She died in a fire when Olivia was eight years old. That's when Olivia came to Alton to live with Nana. She doesn't talk much about what happened during the fire. But she did tell me a ghost woke her up, and it was too late to save her mother.

Photos of Olivia are also on the wall, and there's even one of me when I was a baby in a frilly dress. Nana died before my first birthday, but Olivia said my great-grandmother got a chance to spoil me.

A four-poster bed is in the center of the room nestled between two nightstands stacked with books. Olivia told me Nana was an avid reader, but she liked to keep her books in her room instead of downstairs in the library.

At the foot of the bed is a steamer trunk. I lift the heavy

lid and find leather journals in different colors and sizes—and I know instantly what they are.

During Nana's lifetime, patrons paid her to contact ghosts, and in these journals, she documented her interactions with both the living and the dead.

Brushing my fingers over the cracked spines, I choose one at random and flip through the pages of Nana's writing. The dates range from 1966 to 1968—not long after Nana moved into the house.

The entries contain details of patrons who wanted to send messages and others who wanted to receive them. For those who asked ghosts to reveal secrets, Nana's compact script documents the details of those revelations, but none in this particular journal are juicy or even interesting to me—most of them revolve around missing heirlooms or hidden money.

For each entry, there's a note of the fee Nana required for her services. Some patrons paid as little as twenty-five dollars, while others paid two to three times as much. For one patron, Nana charged over a thousand dollars.

I wonder if Nana had any remorse about taking money from her patrons. Olivia told me some people in Alton thought Nana was a fake, but I've always thought maybe they didn't like that she turned her gift into a profitable business.

I pause at an entry dated May 14, 1967. A patron named Wilma Crawford traveled from Nashville to ask Nana about the afterlife so she could prepare for it.

> *This poor woman was so disappointed in my answer, but I refuse to lie. I cannot tell her what to expect. When I access my Lodestar to enter the spirit realm, it is specific only to me.*

The spirit realm is the place beyond our physical plane and beyond death. Once a ghost enters the spirit realm, they can't be contacted. It's the reason why Olivia can't communicate with her mother or even with Nana. We can only speak to the dead on this physical plane.

I've always known Lodestars to be a place of protection. My own Lodestar took me to a blank void, but Nana used hers to enter the spirit realm. If this was true, my great-grandmother could enter the afterlife and summon the dead.

I read the journal entry again. How did Nana's Lodestar help her travel to the afterlife? Was it possible because of her lifelong gift? None of the ghosts I've met could tell me about the spirit realm, and the ones who crossed over couldn't return.

Dark memories fill my brain as I think of the last ghost I encountered. A lump in my throat rises as I try to push the thoughts away, but I find myself swooshed into the Arizona forest staring up at the tree-lined sky. The wicked ghost changing into its true form—a decaying corpse with rotting teeth. The pressure inside my chest. The bright light of my Lodestar leading me to safety, and then returning to my body to see Olivia's frantic face hovering over me.

My Lodestar saved me from the wicked ghost that night, but maybe this power could take me to the spirit realm too.

But even the thought of speaking with the dead makes my body tremble with anxiety. I don't know if I still want to honor the family tradition. And if I lose my gift soon, it will mean the spirit realm would remain a mystery to me until my own death.

Closing Nana's journal, I put it back with the others and close the steamer trunk.

Morning sunlight filters into my room, and I stretch wide. Now that Olivia isn't sleeping next to me like she did in the RV, it's nice having an entire bed of my own.

I take the back stairs to the kitchen. Olivia is putting veggie omelets on plates, and I sit at the kitchen island as she pours a glass of orange juice for me.

"I need to go downtown for art supplies," she says.

"You want me to come with you?"

"I think you should have a look around the neighborhood. You can go to the park. Maybe you'll meet some of the kids who go to your school."

The thought of meeting anyone gives me a tremble of nerves, but I eat my omelet without protest. After washing our dishes and cleaning up the kitchen, we go outside and walk to the gate. On the curb, Olivia gives me a quick kiss before she leaves.

The street is quiet as I wander with no particular destination. Most of the houses are painted white, while others are pale blue or different hues of yellow. Some houses have green shutters. Others have red doors. One house is painted all black.

"Now this is what a haunted house should look like." I pull out my phone and take several photos.

I walk the length of Noble Avenue to the neighborhood park. Toddlers are playing in a sandbox, and other kids are laughing on swings. Parents sit on benches, their conversations hanging in the Sunday morning air. So far, there's nothing unusual about my new neighborhood, and I haven't felt the presence of any ghosts. Maybe Nana's house is the only haunted one.

When I leave the park and return to Noble Avenue, I start to develop brighter thoughts. On my block, I spot the girl I saw yesterday from my window.

In the morning sun, the girl's hair is lighter than I first thought—more brown than black. Her legs are lanky and tan, and she's wearing overall shorts with a red T-shirt.

The girl hasn't noticed me, so I quicken my pace to Nana's house, hoping I won't have to interact with her—but before I make it to the gate, she looks directly at me.

Heat rushes to my face. I could ignore her and go inside, but I know that would be rude. Also, if she goes to Noble Middle School, I'll see her at school tomorrow anyway, so I might as well introduce myself now.

Reluctantly, I cross the street to the sidewalk in front of her yard. The girl slowly stands and opens her mouth but then closes it as if she's changed her mind about talking to me. My face starts to burn again.

"Hi, I'm Wednesday. I just moved here from . . ." I stop because the RV didn't have an actual address, so I think of the place where Olivia and I spent most of our time. "I moved here from Las Vegas. I'll be going to Noble Middle School. Is that where you go?"

"You can see me," the girl says.

"Of course I can—"

A car horn startles me, and I look across the street. Olivia has returned from her downtown errands. She gives me a happy wave before getting out of the car with her bags.

When I turn back around, the girl is gone.

I frantically search the porch, and the hairs on my arms stand up when I realize what's happened. Some ghosts flicker like glitchy holograms. Others are transparent like fading mirages. But certain kinds of ghosts have solid forms.

The girl who just disappeared into thin air was like that—she wasn't a living person at all.

I bolt across the street, moving past Olivia with her bags. By the time I reach the gate, my heart is thundering in my chest.

"I stopped by the beauty supply store," Olivia says from behind me. "You want me to put new braids in for your first day of school?"

"Okay," I answer, trying to keep the panic out of my voice.

I stay calm as we enter the house, but then I rush up the staircase to my room. I lean against the door, close my eyes, and start counting. When I get to thirty-seven, I feel safe again.

After two long, deep breaths, I slowly walk to the window and peek through the lace curtains at the house across the street.

The ghost is nowhere to be seen.

CHAPTER FOUR

Olivia drives me to school for my first day, even though it's walking distance from Nana's house. She fusses with my fresh braids while we wait in the drop-off line.

"Everything is going to be fine," she says.

I gently push her nervous hands from my hair. Last night she braided in the two bundles she brought home. When Olivia said the color combination would show school spirit, I rolled my eyes. But now I love how the blue and gold braids glint in the morning sun.

"Don't worry, first-day jitters are normal." Olivia keeps talking. "If you need help, just look for a friendly face."

I haven't told her about the ghost across the street yet. After dinner I camped out at my window and waited with a mix of fear and curiosity, but the girl never made an appearance. I'm still not sure if I'm disappointed or relieved.

We pull up to the drop-off point, and I get out of the car. "You don't have to pick me up," I quickly tell Olivia. "I can walk back to the house after school."

"Are you sure, Wednesday?"

When I nod, she blows a kiss and drives away. I walk

through the school's courtyard and try to ignore the nervous energy spinning in my stomach, but none of the kids are staring. Most of them don't notice me as I travel around their clusters of friends to the main entrance.

Inside the school, the halls rumble with the white noise of voices and lockers slamming. A rush of anxiety hits me when I realize I don't know a single living soul at this school. What if everyone hates me? What if someone makes fun of my name? What if I can't find a friendly face?

A sheen of sweat appears on my forehead and worry swims in my chest. I try to conquer the approaching doom with deep breaths, but it doesn't help.

That's when I see the ghost.

He's wearing a green windbreaker and jeans. His brown skin is faded and his body wavers when unknowing students move through him.

I quickly turn and walk in the opposite direction until I see a sign for the bathroom and push open the door. Panting, I dart into the first stall.

"Of course this school is haunted," I whisper loudly. "What did you expect?"

I adjust my clothes and gently pull out the braids tangled in my backpack straps.

The boy in the hallway is a wisp ghost. They replay the same scenario over and over. Never diverging or changing. They're never aware of the living. Harmless.

I let this fact calm me, but then my thoughts spiral

again. "Okay, you need to get a grip because you know he's not the only ghost."

When I open the stall door, I gape at a girl standing at one of the sinks. I didn't see her when I stormed into the bathroom and hid in the stall.

Her fixed stare confirms she's heard everything I've just said, and I fight the urge to huddle back into the stall and disappear forever. Awkwardly, I move forward to the sink beside her and start washing my hands.

I make a point not to make eye contact, but when I finally look up, she locks eyes with me in the mirror. She has dark brown skin and her thick hair is styled in two coily buns. The blue-and-gold outfit she's wearing looks like she's on some kind of spirit squad. I debate if I should say anything to explain myself, but she speaks first.

"Are you new here?"

"First day." I let out a nervous laugh. "I'm Wednesday Thomas."

"Wednesday? Like the goth girl from that show?" Her face lights up. "She can't dance to save her life, but I love her."

"Not that one," I say. "The original one—my mother was obsessed with Wednesday Addams growing up."

"I'm Alexa Scott." She pauses as if she wants to ask me something else, but then the bell saves me. "I should get to homeroom."

Alexa turns to leave, but before she reaches the door, she turns around with a concerned expression.

"Wednesday, since you're new here, I have some advice for you: if you don't want to be known as a weirdo in this school, you shouldn't talk to yourself in the bathroom unless you know you're alone."

My morning is uneventful after seeing the wisp ghost, and despite my fears, Noble Middle School does have many friendly faces. No one makes fun of any name, and I realize I'm slightly ahead in my classes. The teachers seem impressed with me except for Ms. Kimball. She gives me the stank eye when I state I've already studied life science, and sunflowers are my favorite angiosperms.

"Don't worry, I think you may still learn something in this class, Miss Thomas," she says as she gives me a syllabus and goes back to the front of the classroom.

"Kimball is an eternal grouch," the girl sitting at the desk next to me says.

Her long black hair is in a French braid, and she's wearing cuffed jeans that show off several ankle bracelets. Her vintage T-shirt looks like it came from one of the shops in Alton's Five Points.

"I *love* your braids," she adds.

"Thanks." My face warms at the compliment.

"Also, I'm Miki Okada. You're Wednesday, right? The new girl from Las Vegas? Did you see *The Menagerie* when Leo Stacks was in it?"

News about me has traveled fast. In homeroom, I decided to tell everyone I was from Las Vegas. Even though I was born right here in Alton, and despite growing up in Boston, Las Vegas has always felt most like my home. I loved how the city welcomed me with its dry heat and bright lights. Olivia also loved creating and selling her art there, so I knew a lot about the casinos, hotels, and shows.

"No, I didn't get a chance to see *The Menagerie* while it ran, but I heard it was good," I tell her.

Miki smiles at me, and it's like a beam of sunshine. Her kindness seems authentic. My chest fills with happy flutters. Is this what making friends feels like?

"You live in the Callahan House, right?" Miki asks.

Anxious energy shoots up my neck. How does she know where I live? I haven't shared that information with anyone yet.

Miki senses my reaction and quickly puts her hands up in defense. "I promise I'm not a creeper. I live a block from your house and saw you moving in this weekend."

My nerves ease up, but barely, and I know it's no use avoiding the truth, since she actually saw me moving into Nana's house. "Yeah, I live there. The house belonged to my great-grandmother."

Miki's eyes grow wide. "You're related to *Josephine Marlow*?"

I swallow at the awe in her voice, and I squirm in my chair. If Miki knows about Nana, then she probably also knows my great-grandmother was a famous medium. At least that's how Nana is remembered in the paranormal circles in Alton.

"I didn't really know her," I quickly say. "She died when I was a baby."

Ms. Kimball clears her throat, and Miki and I both straighten up in our seats. I don't need to give the Grouch of Science a reason to dislike me more than she already does.

Miki gives me another wide smile, but now my happy flutters of possible friendship have disappeared.

CHAPTER FIVE

I gather my courage as I enter the cafeteria, but it quickly disappears after I get my lunch tray. Every seventh grader turns and stares at me, and I want to shrink away from the attention.

I see Alexa sitting at a table full of other members of the spirit squad. She glances up at me, but she doesn't make any moves to invite me to eat lunch with her.

My palms are sweating, and my backpack feels like a boulder pressing on my spine. Everyone is waiting for the new girl to make a decision. One that will define who I am at this school.

The weight of this choice creates a thundercloud in my brain. What if I sit at the wrong table? What if I sit at a table and everyone gets up and leaves? What if eating in the cafeteria is a mistake?

My tray wobbles in my hands. The last thing I need is to drop it in front of everyone. When the choice becomes too overwhelming and I decide to sit at an empty table in the far corner, a voice calls my name.

Miki waves at me from one of the high-top tables. She's sitting with a light-skinned girl with curly brown hair who's in my first-period math class. It takes me a few moments to remember the girl's very Southern name: Danni-Lynn Porter.

I'm still wary of Miki since she knows where I live, but no one else has invited me to sit with them. The rest of the seventh grade has already gone back to ignoring me, so I reluctantly walk to their table.

"How's your first day so far?" Miki asks.

"Okay, I guess."

"It can be hard being the new girl after school starts," Miki says. "But it's only been a month, so you haven't missed much."

"I can't believe you didn't see *The Menagerie*—not even once," Danni-Lynn says in a dramatic drawl. "If I lived in Vegas, I would have gone *every* night."

"Danni-Lynn is a superfan of Leo Stacks," Miki casually tells me. "That's the only reason she cares about the show."

"Anyway, it doesn't matter. Leo's back in London now," Danni-Lynn playfully pouts. "At least we were in the same country for an *entire* summer."

"Separated by thousands of miles and three time zones," Miki says. "I don't know why you're so obsessed with that British boy. Wednesday, do you know she's made me watch *Loveburned* at least six times now? I know every episode by heart."

"Don't act like you didn't love all those kissing scenes, and the way Leo fights those bullies for messing with his boyfriend."

"Okay, I do like boys who can kiss *and* fight," Miki agrees.

"Leo also has the face and voice of an actual angel. Imagine seeing him on stage in all his glory." Danni-Lynn shimmies in her seat, and her brown curls bounce with her excitement.

Miki shakes her head. "You're so hopeless."

"Mama couldn't get tickets, but just know I would have been in the front row, and then they would have to roll me out in a stretcher when the show was over!"

"Ambulance and full CPR for you," Miki laughs.

I watch the girls tease each other, but Miki and Danni-Lynn don't seem like they would be friends at all. Danni-Lynn seems too much like the debutante type. The kind who wears white gloves, eats cucumber sandwiches, and drinks sweet tea. Even now, she's overdressed for school wearing linen pants, a pink ruffled blouse, and an actual strand of pearls. Miki reminds me a lot of Olivia just from her artsy clothes. Maybe she's also a free spirit who loves indie music, writes angry poetry, and makes protest signs.

Thankfully, Miki hasn't mentioned Nana's haunted house. My stomach has settled down, and the tension has left my shoulders. There's no brewing hurricane in my brain. Maybe I've sat at the right table after all.

Then I take a bite of a chicken nugget.

"It's horrible, right?" Miki laughs. "Barbecue sauce makes it less disgusting."

She gives me one of her packets of sauce, which only

masks the nasty taste of the nuggets. But the roasted potatoes aren't bad, and I have faith the banana will be good.

"Why did you move to Alton?" Danni-Lynn asks.

"My mother grew up here, and she thought it would be a good idea to enroll me in school," I tell her. "We've been traveling in an RV, and she homeschooled me."

Miki looks impressed. "That sounds incredible."

"Sometimes I wish I was homeschooled," Danni-Lynn says quietly.

Miki gives her a reassuring smile, but Danni-Lynn doesn't say anything more.

"Homeschool is actually kind of boring," I tell her.

Danni-Lynn's bright mood has dimmed, and Miki doesn't say anything to fill up the silence.

As I try to think of a different topic for conversation, a woman wanders into the cafeteria. Her pale cheeks are flushed pink as if she's just come in from the cold. Glossy brown hair falls in waves around her shoulders, and the hem of a bloodstained dress flutters underneath her yellow peacoat.

My classmates can't see the woman moving around the tables. They don't know she's leaning over them and listening. At some tables she laughs in glee, but at others, her forehead wrinkles in concern.

I freeze when the woman in the yellow peacoat looks in my direction and our eyes meet. An alertness draws up in her face, and I let out a soft gasp.

She knows I can see her.

The woman is a guide ghost. They like helping other ghosts on this plane. They also love mingling with the living—especially those who can see them.

I know this woman will want to talk to me, and then she'll want me to help all the other ghosts she knows.

The cafeteria falls away and the night in the Arizona state park flashes before me like a nightmare. The wicked ghost hovering in the air before scattering apart into slivers of darkness. The deep fear of the cold crushing my heart. I push away the awful memories and force myself back to the bright Noble Middle School cafeteria.

The woman frantically waves her arms at me as if I need help seeing her. My heartbeat accelerates. What if she's not a guide ghost at all? What if she's wicked? What if she wants to hurt me?

When the ghost walks toward me, I bolt up from the high-top table. My chair crashes to the floor and makes a terrible, loud noise. Other classmates look at me strangely.

"Wednesday? Are you okay?" Miki asks.

I don't want to talk to the woman in the yellow peacoat. I still remember the dark, star-filled sky. The weight on my chest, and the air being sucked out of my lungs. The overwhelming weakness and utter hopelessness.

Miki touches my arm. "Wednesday, do you see something?"

My classmates are now pointing at me and whispering, but my total focus is on the ghost. The woman in the yellow peacoat is moving toward me, and I can't let her get too close. Too close and she'll grab me. Too close and I'll be hurt.

"Hello? Hello! Can you hear me? Yes! Yes, you can!"

When I hear the ghost's voice, my panic tilts over. All the fear I've been holding inside finally unleashes.

"Stay away from me!" I yell and then run out of the cafeteria.

I sprint down the hallway until I'm sure the ghost hasn't followed me. It's not until I slow down and catch my breath that I feel the utter embarrassment of what's happened. I close my eyes to stop angry tears from falling.

Miki runs to where I'm standing. "I told Mrs. Linston I would check on you," she says after catching her breath.

An older dark-skinned woman in a red cardigan appears from around the corner. "Miki, is that girl all right?"

"Everything is under control, Mrs. Linston," Miki says.

The teacher gives us a long look as if she's not convinced, but then she shakes her head and returns to the cafeteria.

Miki gives me my backpack. "I brought your stuff so you wouldn't have to see everyone again."

I slowly take it from her. "Thanks."

Miki leans against the wall next to me but doesn't say anything else. Maybe she thinks I'm going to explain my behavior. Or maybe she wants me to tell her what I saw that made me bolt out of the cafeteria.

"Are you okay?" she asks.

"I'm fine. This whole thing is just kind of embarrassing. I wanted to keep a low profile on my first day."

"Well, that didn't happen." Miki lets out a small giggle. "Sorry."

"No, you're right," I say with a weary laugh. "I'm very high profile now."

Miki leans closer to me. "If I didn't know any better, I'd think you saw a ghost."

An uneasy gurgle plops in my stomach. I don't want to tell her about the woman in the yellow peacoat.

"No, forget it," Miki quickly says. "But . . . you saw something? Right?"

The bell rings, and the classroom doors open. Students spill out into the hallway, but Miki ignores them and studies my face, waiting for a response.

I could lie and say I didn't see a ghost in the cafeteria. I could blame everything on the chicken nuggets, but bad food doesn't cause hallucinations.

Maybe I could just tell her the truth, but I know I can't do that.

"I should get to my next class," I say.

CHAPTER SIX

The rest of the day is very awkward after seeing the guide ghost. Instead of friendly faces, I get weird stares. Now everyone in Noble Middle School knows who I am: Wednesday Thomas, the new girl who lost it in the cafeteria.

My last class is gym, and everyone in the locker room openly whispers about me. I try my best to ignore them, but I have to admit the not-so-quiet conversations make my stomach ache and tight knots of worry burrow into my shoulders.

Alexa glances at me as the other girls talk around her, but she remains silent as she changes into her gym clothes.

Coach Glover announces we're doing laps to determine our baseline fitness. While the other girls groan, my heart leaps in hallelujah because running isn't a team sport. I can be alone and away from the gossip.

On the field, I wonder if the guide ghost in the cafeteria knows about the others who haunt the school. Maybe the woman knows the name of the wisp ghost I saw in the hallway this morning. I quickly shake my head and run faster, because I shouldn't be thinking about the dead.

After I finish my laps, Coach Glover makes a note of my time on her clipboard. "Good job, Wednesday. You should think about joining one of our sports teams."

I give her a humble grin, and she tells me I can go change. The locker room is empty, and I quickly shower and put my clothes back on. When the door opens, I'm surprised to see it's Alexa.

She looks around to make sure we're alone before she speaks. "You didn't listen to what I told you in the bathroom."

When I give her a confused look, she lets out an amused huff. "You shouldn't have run out of the cafeteria. Now everybody thinks you're a weirdo. But don't worry, soon there'll be some other drama, and they'll forget about it."

Alexa is popular and looks like the queen-bee type from the movies—the boy-crazy kind who loves fashion and leads a pack to terrorize girls like me. But she hasn't told anyone what she witnessed this morning in the bathroom.

"Why do you care? You don't even know me," I tell her.

Alexa widens her eyes in disbelief. "I'm trying to help you, Wednesday. There's still enough time for you to act normal."

"You—you think people are going to forget I'm a weirdo?"

"Only if you don't pull any more stunts," Alexa says as she crosses her arms against her chest. "Also, I have some more advice: you might want to find some new friends. Miki and Danni-Lynn are the *last* people you need right now."

"What's wrong with them?"

The door opens again, and the other girls from gym class spill into the locker room. Alexa quickly turns away as if we weren't having a conversation at all. When she joins a group of girls going to the showers, she walks past me as if I don't even exist.

After the school day ends, I go hide in the bathroom stall and wait for the buses to leave. I'm too exhausted to handle any more gawking or whispering.

When I creep out into the hallway, I'm rewarded with blissful silence—even the wisp ghost isn't wandering around.

Only a few students linger in the school courtyard. None of them are paying me any attention, but then I see Miki and Danni-Lynn sitting at a stone table under a shade of trees. Danni-Lynn waves at me, and I hesitate for a moment before waving back at her.

"I've been so worried about you!" she yells across the courtyard. "Are you okay?"

I wince when two seventh-grade boys glance my way, and one of them points at me and laughs.

"No need to worry about me! Everything is fine," I yell back in a too-cheery voice.

Miki gets up from the table and motions for Danni-Lynn to follow her. My heart gives a jolt of alarm when they trot across the courtyard to greet me.

"We're going to get cupcakes. Do you want to come with us?" Miki offers.

"The Beloved Bakery's cupcakes are so good, they taste like a sin," Danni-Lynn adds. "You have to try one!"

A cupcake would be well deserved after the day I've had, and if I showed up at Lincoln's bakery, he would be happy to see me. Especially if I arrived with new friends.

But then I remember what happened in the cafeteria with the guide ghost, and the way I overreacted. Miki already suspects I saw something. Maybe this cupcake invitation is just an opportunity for her to ask me more questions. Alexa has already warned me to stay away from Miki and Danni-Lynn, although she didn't get a chance to tell me why.

"Thanks, but I'm kind of tired," I tell them.

"Oh, okay." Miki's shoulders droop in defeat. "Maybe another time?"

"You should go get some rest, Wednesday." Danni-Lynn gently pats me on the back like I'm eighty instead of twelve.

When the girls get a good distance away, Miki starts using her hands as she talks, and Danni-Lynn nods furiously. They playfully bump shoulders, and their faint laughter travels back to me.

I continue to stare at them and feel a sharp longing in my chest. When I'm the only one left in the school courtyard, I let out a deep sigh and start my walk alone to Nana's house.

"Wednesday, is that you?"

Surprised, I follow Jasmine's voice to the library and find her sitting behind the massive desk. She's hunched over a laptop, but she straightens up when she sees me.

"Hey, Jasmine, what are you doing here?"

"Welcome to my new office!" She beams at me. "I'm going to use this space for the semester. I also wanted to spend time with Olivia, but so far, she's staying up in that turret being a mad artist."

Jasmine has already put some of her books and a collection of shiny rocks on the bookshelves. I slide my backpack off my shoulders and let it hit the floor with a heavy thud before I collapse into one of the leather chairs.

"First day of school that bad?" Jasmine asks.

"It could have been worse, but it could have been much, much better. Noble Middle School is definitely haunted. I should have known that, but it still freaked me out."

"I can see how that would make your first day challenging." Jasmine raises her eyebrows in acknowledgment. "Did you meet any nice *living* folks today?"

"I had lunch with two girls," I mumble.

Jasmine gives me a hopeful look. "Oh, that's good. Right?"

"I've never really had friends before," I confess. "It's always been just me and Olivia."

Jasmine leans forward and several gold bangles clink together on her light brown arms. Her hazel eyes are dark in the low light of the room. "Making friends is hard. I mean, your mama and I only became friends because she gave me free cupcakes."

"What?" I let out a surprised laugh. "Olivia never told me this."

Jasmine smiles at me before she loses herself to the past. "I think she knew I wasn't the happiest person back then. I had sharp edges. For whatever reason, Liv liked me and those cupcakes were *good*, so I kept going back to the bakery."

I knew about Jasmine's childhood. Her mother struggled with addiction, and Jasmine spent time in and out of foster care. Despite all this, Jasmine graduated high school at sixteen. That's when she came to Alton to attend the university on full scholarship. Olivia was working the register at the Beloved Bakery when they first met. Then Jasmine fell in love with Lincoln and they became a couple. After she graduated, Jasmine never left, and now she's the youngest professor in the geology department.

"Olivia says you'll always be best friends. I want something like that . . . but I'm not sure how to even go about it."

"What about the two girls you had lunch with today?"

I shrug at the possibility. No need to share the actual details of my lunch with Miki and Danni-Lynn—I don't want to relive that drama.

"Listen, I'm not gonna lie to you. You're the new girl and everyone already has their established friend groups." Jasmine pauses. "I don't want you to force anything or get mistreated just because you don't want to be alone. Promise me you'll make good choices."

I stare into her eyes and see the fierce love she has for me. "Okay, I promise."

CHAPTER SEVEN

I do my homework at the desk Olivia brought down from the turret's storage room. It's a sturdy antique with a nice flat writing surface—a Callahan heirloom left behind in the house. I hope Caleb doesn't mind I'm using it, but I guess he'll let me know soon enough if he does.

I think about all the ghosts I've encountered so far in Alton—the girl across the street, the boy in the school hallway, and the woman in the cafeteria. Ignoring the dead is harder than I thought it would be, but at least none of them has tried to hurt me.

The neighborhood lampposts have turned on and shadows of trees dance on the hardwood floor. I turn off the lights and go to my window. When I peek through the lace curtains, the girl across the street is standing in her yard and looking right at me.

I duck away as if I've been caught doing something wrong, but then I slowly take another peek. The ghost hasn't moved. After a few seconds, the girl waves at me and then goes to sit on her porch.

My breath hitches. Is she waiting for me? Does she

want to talk to me? Should I go see her? I bite my lip as curiosity churns in my stomach.

I decide not to overthink it. I scramble down the staircase before I lose my nerve. The evening air is humid, so I take one of the hair ties I always keep on my wrist and put my braids in a loose ponytail.

The porch light is off, so the house across the street is dark, but I can see the girl sitting on the steps. I walk down to the gate, and it opens with a low, muted creak. My heartbeat thrums in my ears as I carefully approach the house draped in shadows until I'm standing in front of the ghost.

"Sorry about yesterday. I didn't know you were . . ." I trail off, not wanting to say the word.

"Dead?" the girl says without remorse.

"How long has it been?"

The girl shrugs. "To be honest, I don't know. Time is strange."

"That's because time doesn't have any meaning for you. Not anymore," I say.

Her dark eyes brim with interest. "How can you see me? No one else can."

"It's a family thing—something I've always been able to do."

The girl now looks at me differently, as if she's identified a special trait in me, but she doesn't say anything.

"What's your name?" I ask.

"Violet Delgado," the girl answers.

"Do you remember how you died?"

Violet frowns for a moment and then furrows her brow like she's trying to remember. "I remember little things—but I don't remember how I died."

"Do you remember living in this house?"

Violet turns her gaze to the dark windows, and my heart breaks a little for the ghost. Jasmine told me a retired couple lives here, and she watches their house while they travel. Right now, the Leehans are in Spain. More than likely Violet's parents are also dead or they've moved away.

"I could help you find out what happened to your parents," I quickly tell her before I can even stop myself.

Violet gives me a look of distrust. "Why would you do that?"

I think about this for a moment. At this point, I already know ignoring the dead is impossible, but the only reason I even decided to do that was because I've been afraid.

Wicked ghosts are rare, and Violet hasn't tried to hurt or possess me. If anything, she seems more afraid of me than I am of her.

I already know I can't keep going around screaming every time I see a ghost, and I don't want to be known as the weirdo of Noble Middle School. But most of all, I don't want to be scared anymore.

Right now, my brain isn't full of lightning—it's calm. Maybe this is how I can conquer my current fear of the dead. I could start with Violet. Maybe we could help each other. She could help me build my trust back with ghosts, and I could help her find out what happened to her parents.

Maybe this is how I can stop the nightmares and flashbacks.

"Violet, let me help you," I say.

When I get back to my room, it doesn't take long to find out what happened to Violet Delgado. After a quick online search on the *Alton Banner-Herald* website, I find her obituary. Violet died of bacterial meningitis just over a year ago.

It takes me longer to find any information about Violet's parents, but I discover one of her mother's social media profiles. The most recent photo is from a month ago. The location tag is Miami, Florida. Violet's mother is holding a newborn baby swaddled in a hospital blanket. Violet's father is in the photo too. She's a mix of both of her parents. Violet has her father's dark eyes and her mother's bright smile. I read the text under the post.

CharlotteDelgado87
My little miracle. Juan Alejandro Martinez Delgado.

I stare at the photo and wonder how Violet will feel about this. Most ghosts are looking for answers, but I'm not sure if this information will give her the peace she's looking for and if it'll be enough for her to move on to the spirit realm. Will she feel discarded and forgotten? Will she be happy about her younger sibling? Will she be jealous? Either way, I'll have to tell Violet what I've found out about her parents.

Out of curiosity, I continue to scroll and look at older photos. Violet's face starts to appear, and I see the girl through her mother's eyes. There's a photo of Violet with a kitten. In another one, Violet is in her bedroom proudly displaying her bookshelves. There's Halloween photos of Violet in a tan jumpsuit holding what looks like a leaf blower—and I realize she's dressed as one of the Ghostbusters. I keep scrolling, but then I stop and lean closer to my laptop.

In the photo, she's wearing a birthday hat and party beads. But I'm not looking at Violet. I'm looking at the other girls who are with her. Miki, Danni-Lynn, and Alexa are hugging Violet in a tight squeeze, cheeks pressed together with wide, happy smiles. I glance at the date of the post—taken a few days before Violet died. I slowly read the text under the photo.

CharlotteDelgado87
Violet and her BFFs.

These girls were best friends, but that definitely isn't the case now. Alexa made that clear when she warned me to stay away from Miki and Danni-Lynn. Something happened after Violet died, and it was strong enough to shatter their friendship.

CHAPTER EIGHT

Dealing with the dead has made me an excellent researcher.

Taking care of unfinished business for ghosts has always required gathering information to uncover answers. I accomplish this by searching for clues online. But in this case, I don't think my laptop will reveal why Alexa stopped being friends with Miki and Danni-Lynn.

I can't ask Violet because ever since I offered to find out what happened to her parents, I haven't seen her. For the last few nights, I've sat at my window and waited for her, but she never shows up.

When another night passes with no sign of Violet, I move the focus of my research from the dead to the living.

One of my theories is Alexa, Miki, and Danni-Lynn didn't become friends with each other on their own—instead Violet brought them all together. Growing up in Boston, I noticed this with other friend circles. There's always one person who's at the center—the best friend to all the others. I knew a group of girls like this. I watched them huddle in the school hallways and at recess. Patricia Hensley was at the center—the hub of a friendship wheel, and the other girls were spinning spokes around her.

Patricia's little sister Tatiana was also a part of the circle, but she went unnoticed because she died the previous year. There was so much Tatiana needed to tell her big sister before she moved on. I already knew Patricia wouldn't believe me, so I left notes in her desk drawer on Tatiana's behalf. I watched as Patricia read them and shifted nervously in her seat before scanning the room. She couldn't see Tatiana standing right beside her, but I could. These notes upset Patricia, which made Tatiana even sadder. It wasn't long afterward that the ghost reluctantly crossed over into the spirit realm without saying goodbye.

Now I wonder if Violet has tried to contact any of her friends. Does she remember being the center of their friendship circle? Does she remember them at all?

Figuring out the connection between the girls hasn't been as easy as I thought it would be. Miki lives in the neighborhood, so maybe that was her connection to Violet, but I don't know where the other girls live, and it doesn't seem like their families would overlap socially. Miki's father is a professor of Asian American studies at the university. Alexa's mother is a commissioner for the city government, and Danni-Lynn's parents—well, her situation is more complicated.

Danni-Lynn's father is a famous university football star, but now he's serving ten years in a state prison for embezzlement. There was a trial in Alton two years ago, and it was covered in both the local and Atlanta newspapers.

In one news video, Danni-Lynn's father is standing with his lawyer, another tall dark-skinned man with a shiny, bald head. Danni-Lynn is standing behind them. Her curly brown hair is decorated with pink ribbons—a style much too young for her. A blond woman who looks like a model is gripping her hand. I recognize her as Danni-Lynn's mother from other news photos. They're both wearing expensive, understated black dresses as if they're in mourning.

"My client is innocent of all charges," the lawyer tells reporters. "We will prove this in our appeal. This is not over."

Although the camera is focused on Tate Porter and his lawyer, my eyes are drawn to Danni-Lynn. She's cowering and trying her best to disappear, which makes me wonder if her parents made her attend the press conference.

Now I understand why Danni-Lynn told me she wanted to be homeschooled. It's probably been awful for her.

But with everything I've uncovered online, I still don't have an obvious connection to why these girls were Violet's best friends.

At school, I continue to observe them from a distance. Alexa avoids talking to me in gym class, but I can tell she approves of me keeping a low profile. It's trickier with Miki. I've made a point to wait until the warning bell to arrive to Ms. Kimball's class so I won't have to sit next to her. The hurt on her face makes my stomach ache. Danni-Lynn still gives me a debutante wave when I see her in the hallways. She doesn't seem to care that I've stopped eating in the cafeteria, or maybe she's being Southern nice.

THE SECRET DEAD CLUB

For the past week, I've been spending my lunch period in the library as I continue to piece together each girl's history. Ms. Cassidy, the school librarian, lets me eat in a study room—mostly because I think she feels sorry for me, but it's the perfect place to do my research.

I eat my sandwich as I turn the pages of the Noble Middle School yearbook from when all the girls were in sixth grade. As expected, Alexa is the most popular and in the most clubs. Spirit squad. Basketball team. Volleyball team. She's even in chorus. Danni-Lynn seems to be the most studious one. She's involved in Science Olympiad, Math Mentoring, and the chess team. Miki appears only once in the yearbook with her class photo, which I find very odd. She seems like the perfect type to be in the Sustainability Corps or even student council, but she's not a member of any club at all.

Turning back a few more pages, I stare at Violet Delgado's class photo. She's wearing a black blouse and her hair is pulled back in a ponytail. I stare into her dark eyes as if I can find the answers to my questions. Like Miki, she isn't listed as a member of any school clubs either—but that's because she died before she could officially join any of them. Underneath her photo, someone has scribbled "RIP."

I startle at the quick knock on the study room door. When a head pokes in, I'm surprised to see Miki's face.

"The library aide told me you were in here."

I quickly close the yearbook and try to cover it up with

my hands, but I know she's already seen it. Miki surveys my scattered notes, but I gather them up before she can read them.

"Why are you looking for me?" I ask.

"I wanted to talk to you." Miki closes the door and then fiddles nervously with her French braid as if she's gathering up courage. "Have I—have I done something wrong?"

I swallow at the hollow crack in her voice. "No, of course not."

Miki hesitates before she moves closer to the table. "But you've been avoiding me. If you tell me what I've done wrong, then I can fix it. I can make sure it never happens again."

Her eyes plead with me, and my face heats up with guilt because she's right. I have been avoiding her, and I haven't given her a reason.

"I'm sorry, it's not you," I say. "It's just been weird since my first day here. I promise, you haven't done anything wrong. There's nothing you need to fix."

Miki blinks and bites her lip. We stare at each other as the silence wraps around us. In the last few days, I've been trying to find out everything I can about this girl—and yet here she is right in front of me, as if my research has summoned her. Instead of playing detective to find the information I need, I could just ask the source right in front of me.

"Actually, there's something I've been meaning to ask you."

Miki's face lights up. "What is it?"

"Do you—did you know Violet Delgado?"

The brightness drains from Miki's eyes. "Where did you hear that name?"

"Oh, I just wondered—"

"How do you know about Violet?"

I stutter at her reaction. "I—I know she lived across the street from me. I just wondered if you had been friends with her?"

Miki's face suddenly fills up with unguarded hope. *"Have you seen her?"*

I swallow, knowing my answer will prove to Miki that she's been right about me. But my curiosity pushes me to truthfully answer her.

"Yes, I asked if she wanted me—"

"Wednesday, stop," Miki interrupts me. "We can't talk about Violet here."

"What—"

"Not here, Wednesday."

"I don't understand—"

"I'll be in touch."

Before I can say anything else, Miki quickly turns away and leaves the study room. My mouth remains open after the door closes.

I lean back in my chair, baffled by what's just happened. The dead are way less confusing than the living.

CHAPTER NINE

When school ends, Miki and Danni-Lynn are waiting for me in the courtyard. Miki's demeanor has totally changed—she's practically giddy. This makes me instantly wary but also extremely curious, so I wait for the girls to approach me.

"Can we talk about Violet now?" I ask.

Miki shakes her head. "Not yet. We don't talk about club business at school."

"We're very strict on that," Danni-Lynn adds in her sweet drawl.

This gets my attention. Maybe this club is the connection I've been looking for all along—the missing piece of the puzzle I've been trying to solve. "Was Violet a member of this club?"

The girls exchange knowing looks, but neither answers me. Instead Miki opens her backpack and pulls out a black envelope.

"I wasn't sure if you would be interested. Especially after what happened in the cafeteria. Then you started to avoid me—which was kind of rude, by the way, but whatever." Miki rolls her eyes. "But after we talked in the library today, I think you might be interested in our club after all."

She gives me the envelope, and I realize it's some kind of invitation. My name is written in glitter ink on the front.

"We prefer you wait until you get home before you open it. Somewhere private, for your eyes only," Miki says.

"Okay," I say slowly.

"We do hope you consider our club," Danni-Lynn says. "You would be a great *asset*."

Both girls look at me with hopeful expectation. Whatever this club is—it has to be the common interest that brought these girls together.

"You're not going to tell me anything else, are you?" I ask.

"You'll see what we mean soon," Miki says. "If you're interested, you'll know where to find us."

When the girls leave me in the school courtyard, I peer down at the black envelope in my hands. Miki's handwriting shimmers in the sunlight. Somber yet playful. Morbid but cheerful.

A tiny spark lights up in my brain with something I didn't put into consideration when I tried to find the connection between the girls, but now it's obvious. Violet lived right across the street from Nana's haunted house, and Miki knows I've seen Violet's ghost.

For a moment, I think about tearing open the black envelope right here in the courtyard to prove my hunch. But I'm not alone, and the last thing I need is another rumor created about me. I don't need to remind anyone I'm a weirdo, so I put the envelope inside my backpack.

When I get to Nana's house, I rush up the staircase to my room and toss my backpack on the bed. I take out the invitation and sit at my desk. Turning it over in my hands, I notice the envelope's weight is heavier than I first realized. If this is an invitation to their club, why couldn't they just ask me? Why did it have to be so formal?

I tear open the envelope. Black glitter sticks to my fingers as it spills out onto the desk. I let out a surprised laugh, because of course Miki would make this as dramatic as possible. I pull out a silver card that glimmers in the afternoon light and stare at the handwritten words.

> Wednesday Thomas, Honored Medium
> You have been cordially invited
> to
> the Dead Club
> (tell absolutely no one about this)

"They can't be serious," I whisper.

Below the invitation is an address with a date and time, but the date has been scratched out with a thick black marker and replaced with the word "TODAY" in bold letters. Miki was ready to invite me to their club last week.

The connection is clear to me now, and it's one I never expected. Miki only asked if I saw a ghost in the cafeteria because she knows I saw one. Alexa didn't tell anyone I thought Noble Middle School was haunted because she already knows it is. Danni-Lynn is also a member of this club, which means she knows all these things too. A question rumbles in my chest: What do they know about Violet?

In the past, I hid my gift because I didn't want to be seen as a freak. I didn't want anyone to be afraid of me. Call me a weirdo or something worse. But despite my best efforts and all my hiding, I didn't make any real friends, and I desperately wanted them.

I've been invited to this club because of who I am. These girls know I can see the dead. They think I would be a great asset. If they aren't afraid of ghosts, then they won't be afraid of me.

The Dead Club is meeting in a half hour. I quickly look up the address on my phone and see it's seven minutes' walking distance. Miki lives in the neighborhood, so the meeting is probably at her house. When I take a deep breath and exhale, black glitter scatters all over my desk. I chuckle at the mess, and at that moment I make my decision.

When I open the door to my room, Olivia is walking down from the turret. She's got on one of the jumpers that she wears when she's working on her art.

"I thought I heard you come in." She stands in front of me and moves braids away from my face. "Want to come up and see what I've been cooking? I'm trying something new with the sheet metal I found."

"I was going to meet with some girls from school."

Olivia's face widens in surprise and then fills up with

disappointment, but she quickly replaces it with a weak smile. "Oh, you've made new friends already? That's wonderful, Wednesday."

The look in her eyes doesn't match the excitement in her voice, and my stomach knots with guilt. For so long, it's been only me and Olivia—but since we've moved to Alton, my world is expanding and her world is shrinking.

"Can I come up and see it when I get back?" I offer.

Olivia squeezes my shoulders and leads us down the staircase. "Of course. Jazzy and Link are coming over for dinner, so I can show y'all my work after we eat."

Now I don't want to leave. Olivia doesn't look happy or sad, but I don't know which emotion she'll choose after I'm gone. She loved living in the RV and traveling the Southwest. After the wicked ghost attacked me, Olivia swiftly left all that behind. She can create art in Nana's house, but I know it isn't the same.

"Did you want to come back to Alton?" I ask. "Is this where you want to be?"

Olivia lets out a heavy sigh as she sits on the bottom step of the staircase. "Honestly, Wednesday, I'm still trying to figure out where I belong. But for now, this house is the best place for you."

The afternoon sun pierces the front door's leaded glass and a prism of light filters over Olivia's face. Should I tell her about my invitation? Does she need to know about the Dead Club? Would Olivia be happy these girls are excited that I can speak with ghosts?

We lock eyes for a moment, and then Olivia gives me a genuine smile, fully showing the love she has for me. The knots in my stomach unravel.

"Wednesday, do you remember what I once told you about my art?"

I nod because I do remember, and I swallow down the lump that's formed in my throat. "You told me I was the most beautiful thing you ever created."

"Beautiful art must be shared." She rises from the staircase and comes to hug me tight. "Go have fun with your friends."

PART TWO
A SECRET CLUB

CHAPTER TEN

Closing the gate, I look across the street, but the porch is empty. No sign of Violet. I try to push away the possibility she may have crossed over—ghosts only linger when there's a need or a reason to stay on this physical plane.

It doesn't take long to get to Hampshire Avenue. Although there aren't any Victorian houses on this block, each home has its own specific character. Miki's house is a white bungalow with a cobblestone walkway leading to a red door. Two hedges hide most of the porch, and ivy crawls along the side of the house. A shaggy black dog watches me from a window, its barking muted by the thick glass. I walk up the brick steps and ring the doorbell.

A tall man in a tennis outfit answers the door and smiles. "You must be Wednesday," he says. "I'm Donnie, Miki's father. Pleasure to meet you."

"Oh—oh, hello," I stutter. "You were expecting me?"

His brown eyes sparkle with kindness. "Miki told me you were coming. They're already out back waiting for you."

I wonder if Miki's father knows about the club and exactly what it's for, but maybe the dead are embraced in this household, and it's no big deal.

"Thanks. Nice meeting you too." I walk down the brick steps and start my way around to the backyard.

Another cobblestone walkway leads to a fancy shed that looks like a tiny model of Miki's house. Black and silver balloons are fastened with ribbons to a small lamppost. Miki seems to like staying on theme, or maybe these are the Dead Club's official colors.

I scratch a nervous tickle on the back of my neck, but I already know it's too late to change my mind. I take off my shoes and place them next to the other two pairs. When I knock, there's muffled scrambling and loud whispers. A few moments later, Miki peers out through a small crack of the door.

"Did you come alone?" she whispers.

I answer with a nod, and Miki closes the door. More loud whispers. I roll my eyes and wait for Miki to invite me in.

The furnished shed has a cream sofa and a green beanbag chair. On the floor is a fluffy rug that's the color of cotton candy. Fairy lights hang over several bookshelves, and a small round table fills up the rest of the space. I don't see any black candles or spooky skulls. It's a cozy place—perfect for reading or watching a movie.

Danni-Lynn waves at me beauty-queen style from the sofa. Miki closes the door and then presents a tray of double–chocolate chip cookies.

"Just so you know, those cookies are *not* from the Beloved Bakery," Danni-Lynn tells me.

"But they're good and homemade." Miki scowls at her. "We have fruit punch too."

I shake my head. "I'm good, thanks."

"We're so glad you decided to come to the meeting." Miki puts the tray on the table and ushers me to the beanbag chair.

"Your father said you were expecting me."

"I wasn't sure you would show up—that was just me manifesting." Miki stretches up to select a paperback from a bookshelf. "Have you ever read this?"

I take it from her and study the cover. There's a girl with a dark aura hovering over a creepy graveyard. I look at the title: *Wait Till Helen Comes*.

"Never heard of it."

Danni-Lynn lets out a sharp gasp of disbelief. "What? It's a ghost story classic. One of Mary Downing Hahn's best."

"Do you want me to read it?"

"It's not required, but highly requested. The club has several copies, so you can borrow that one if you want," Danni-Lynn tells me.

I look back down at the cover, and a tiny spark of unease stirs in my brain. I now realize the girl on the cover is a ghost, but her eyes are dark and devious. Wicked.

"To become a club member, you have to take the oath on *Helen*," Miki tells me. "But this isn't an official meeting, so no oath will be taken today. You can think of this as a meet and greet to see if the club is a good fit for you."

Miki sits beside Danni-Lynn on the sofa, and the two

girls stare at me. The room fills with stiff silence.

I place the paperback on the small round table. "Maybe we should get to the point. You invited me here because you think I can see the dead."

"You did see Ms. Tarkington in the cafeteria," Miki says in a matter-of-fact tone.

I fidget in the beanbag chair. Laura Tarkington is the guide ghost who made me freak out in front of the entire seventh grade.

"You did see her, right?" Danni-Lynn's eyes are bright and hopeful.

I uncovered information about the guide ghost during my research. Laura Tarkington's cause of death was easy to find online.

"She was a teacher who got hit by a car last year," I tell them. "But it happened downtown, not at the school. How—how do you know she haunts the cafeteria?"

The girls look at each other for a moment, secrets bouncing between them. Miki smiles in smug satisfaction.

"What about Terrance Sims?" she asks. "Have you seen him in the hallways?"

I blink slowly. Was that the wisp ghost's name? The boy in the green windbreaker? I wasn't able to find any information about him because I didn't know where to start.

"Is this some kind of test?" I hate that my voice tilts too high in defense.

"No, not a test," Danni-Lynn reassures me. "We already know you can see ghosts."

I realize Alexa isn't here at this meeting. Is this the

reason she told me to stay away from Miki and Danni-Lynn? Because of this Dead Club? My brain churns with the possibility.

"Are there more members?" I ask.

Miki gives me a nervous look. "This isn't an official meeting, and we take the confidentiality of our other members very seriously."

Her answer doesn't give me much to go on, but there's still a chance Alexa could be a member, although the odds seem slim, considering her behavior.

"Okay, I get it. Privileged membership," I say, trying to ignore how the curiosity surges in my brain like an electric storm.

Miki gives me a grateful smile, and Danni-Lynn sighs in relief. Both girls are happy that I'm not pressing them about other members.

"What else do you want to know about me?" I ask them. "Anything specific?"

Miki leans over and whispers into Danni-Lynn's ear, and she nods before speaking.

"The most important thing is that you're *willing* to communicate with the dead," Danni-Lynn tells me. "It has to be something you *want* to do."

I squirm again in the beanbag chair, which makes me sink deeper into it. Did I want to communicate with ghosts, or did I want to ignore them? My change of heart happened because of Violet Delgado, the dead girl across the street who I wanted to help. A ghost who may have already crossed over to the spirit realm.

"Ghosts talk to me only if they want—I can't make them," I say.

"Fair enough," Miki says. "But if you feel this is something that you want to do, then you may be a good fit for our club. We definitely need a medium."

"We'll give you some time to think about it," Danni-Lynn says. "We'll be in touch soon."

Both girls rise from the sofa to signal the end of the meeting, but I remained seated.

"Wait . . . that's it? You don't want to know what Violet said to me?"

Danni-Lynn's eyes widen. *"You've seen Violet?"*

"Miki didn't tell you?" I pause. "I thought that was the reason I was here."

Miki winces at Danni-Lynn's glare. "I was going to tell you in our next officer meeting."

Danni-Lynn rises from the sofa, her eyes full of irritation. "You better tell me everything."

"I promise." Miki wrings her hands nervously.

More questions brim in my chest. Have they been trying to contact Violet? Why was Miki being so *secretive*? Now the Dead Club knows more about me, and I barely know anything about Violet.

Both girls escort me to the door, and the expressions on their faces tell me the meet-and-greet session is officially over.

Unless Violet makes another appearance, this club may be the only way I'll ever get any answers.

CHAPTER ELEVEN

When I get back to Nana's house, Olivia and Jasmine are in the kitchen. Olivia is mixing salad in a bowl, and Jasmine is draining pasta in the sink. Old-school music plays from a speaker on the kitchen island.

"Did you have fun with your new friends?" Olivia asks.

"It was okay," I say, washing my hands. "Need me to help with anything?"

"You can grate some parmesan," Jasmine offers.

I pull the block of cheese from the fridge. Olivia stirs sauce at the stove and belts out the chorus to En Vogue's "Free Your Mind." Jasmine makes a gagging face at Olivia's bad singing and leans against the kitchen island next to me.

"Are these new friends the same ones you had lunch with on your first day?"

"Yeah, same girls."

She grins at me, approving of this development. What would Jasmine think about Miki and Danni-Lynn wanting me to be the medium for their club? She's been taking care of Nana's haunted house for years, so maybe she would think it's a bonus to have friends like this. But I decide not to tell her about the black envelope full of glitter or the secret meeting.

Lincoln walks into the kitchen with a turquoise Beloved Bakery box. "I brought cupcakes!"

Jasmine grabs the box out of his hands. "Do you have strawberry in here?"

"Saved one for you." Lincoln leans down and kisses Jasmine's forehead.

After we eat spaghetti and salad on the sunporch, we follow Olivia up to the turret, where she shows us her latest mixed-media project.

"I have a lot of work left to do," she says.

Olivia has transformed sheet metal into various geometric shapes and molded other pieces into delicate leaves and petals. She's painted the canvas in blue and yellow shades and added black calligraphy. On the worktable next to the easel, pieces of sheet metal are in different stages of creation—small twirls, fancy etchings, and thick patterns.

Jasmine moves closer to the artwork and gently touches a metallic petal. "It's so beautiful."

We continue to admire Olivia's canvas and marvel how art can be made from things that have been discarded—how beauty can be revealed with transformation. Olivia has always seen the creative potential in things that others have thrown away. This is her true gift.

Jasmine kisses my cheek before she leaves with Lincoln, and Olivia begins to clean her workspace and organize the scraps of sheet metal.

I walk to the turret window. It's right above my room, and I can see the house across the street. The Leehans haven't returned from Spain, so the rooms are empty and dark.

"You told Jazzy your school is haunted," Olivia says from behind me. "Does that mean you can still see spirits?"

I turn away from the window. "A few. Not many."

Olivia's face fills up with careful consideration. "I wasn't sure if you could see them. Are you okay?"

"They scared me at first," I admit, turning back to the window. "There's one across the street."

Olivia approaches me, and I see our reflections in the dark glass. Her mirror twin pushes my braids from my face. "Tell me about this spirit."

"Her name is Violet—she died a year ago, but she doesn't remember much of her life. Not even how she died."

"Did she ask you for help?"

"Not exactly, but I offered to find out what happened to her parents. I—I haven't seen her again to tell her about them."

Olivia's reflection changes in the window. She presses her lips together and bubbling dread brews in my stomach.

"It starts off slow," she says gently. "Fades in and out at first. Sometimes I could see spirits, but then other times I couldn't. Then one day, I couldn't see them at all and never saw them again."

I turn to face the flesh-and-blood Olivia and see the possible truth reflected in her eyes. I told her I would be *ready* when my gift faded, but that was when I wanted to ignore the dead.

Over the past week, I've been so distracted by the living that I've taken my gift for granted.

Now I'm not sure if I can see ghosts at all.

I turn and stare at the dark house across the street. What if Violet hasn't moved on? What if she's looking at me right now? What if she's been waiting for *me* all this time?

If I can't see ghosts anymore, then I can't be the Dead Club's medium, and I can't help Violet either. I won't be able to help any ghosts. Not anymore.

Olivia gently guides my chin to her face so she can look at me again. "Wednesday, if your gift is fading, you should be proud of all you've done. The spirits are grateful."

A small storm erupts in my brain, but this commotion of unease is from the fear of what I may lose forever. I blink back the sharp bite of tears. How could I tell Olivia that now I didn't *want* to lose my gift?

The anxiety continues to build in my body, and I fight the urge to run down the staircase, push through the gate, and rush out into the street. With the humid weight of the night air on my skin, I would scream loud enough for every ghost in Alton to hear me. Loud enough to let them know I'm still here.

I turn away from Olivia, not wanting to accept the reality of what could be happening to me. There's nothing I can do to stop my gift from fading. Not even if now more than ever, I desperately want to see the dead.

CHAPTER TWELVE

I stand in the school hallway and watch the wisp ghost. Terrance Sims doesn't notice me, and he wavers like smoke every time a student passes through him.

This time the ghost doesn't rattle me. He doesn't trigger any anxiety or sense of dread. Now that I see him fully, his face is full of joy. It was a good day for him—and that memory is imprinted in this space.

When the hallway clears after the warning bell, I move closer and reach out to touch him, but only cold air meets my fingers. It's the same chill my classmates feel when they move through him—even if they don't know it's the reason they shiver. They don't know it's a memory of a boy in a green windbreaker on one of the happiest days of his life.

My return to the cafeteria doesn't cause a commotion. No one notices or stares at me except for Alexa. We lock eyes for a moment, but then she averts her gaze and returns her attention to the other girls sitting at her table.

When I approach Miki and Danni-Lynn, I give them a small wave before joining them at the high-top table.

"Don't worry, I remember," I quickly say. "No club business at school."

Miki smiles knowingly at me. "We appreciate it."

I pull out my lunch and then scan the cafeteria. I don't have to wait long for Laura Tarkington to appear in her yellow peacoat. The teacher's cheeks are forever pink from the cold day she died. The blood splattered on the hem of her dress is still bright red. I watch as she moves around the tables and leans over students. This time, there's no swirling storm inside me—only a flooding relief that I can see the guide ghost.

"Have you decided what you're going to wear for your yearbook picture?" Danni-Lynn asks me. "You missed picture day last month, but they usually do retakes in November."

I pull my gaze away from the ghost. "I'll probably just wear one of my T-shirts and some jeans."

"Wednesday, this picture will be in the yearbook. *Forever.* And you can't take it back once it's in there. If you get famous, everyone will see it."

"I don't plan on becoming famous."

Danni-Lynn laughs. "That's what Leo Stacks thought before he got discovered and cast in *Loveburned*. Now he's got five million followers. All his school pictures are tragic, and I know he hates they exist. You need to take this seriously, Wednesday."

"You should wear something to match your braids," Miki suggests. "Or do you plan to put in a different color?"

"Do you own any cute dresses?" Danni-Lynn asks. "I haven't seen you wear any to school. You could borrow one of mine if you want."

"Danni-Lynn has plenty of dresses, but I hope you like sequins," Miki jokingly warns.

"Now you know I have the good sense not to give Wednesday one of my pageant dresses."

"I don't want to wear a dress," I say, staring at the guide ghost.

Laura Tarkington has noticed me, but she doesn't approach my table. She remains standing near a group of seventh-grade boys making a tower of empty milk cartons. Her eyes are curious, but she doesn't move. The guide ghost is waiting to see if I'm going to yell at her again.

I put my sandwich quickly back in my lunch bag. "I need to leave."

Miki slowly follows my gaze and squints at the table of boys as one of them knocks over the milk-carton tower amid a shower of loud complaints.

"Do you see her?" she whispers.

I nod as I put my lunch bag into my backpack. "I should probably take this outside."

This time when I get up from the table, I don't knock over my chair and make a loud commotion. No one in the cafeteria notices—except for Alexa, who's watching me with an intense curiosity.

I'm not sure if the guide ghost still wants to talk to me, but it's probably a safer bet than having a conversation here out in the open in the cafeteria—that didn't go too well last time.

I approach the patio doors and with a quick tilt of my head, I invite Laura Tarkington to follow me outside.

On the patio, I sit at an empty table in the far corner with my back to the cafeteria doors, nibbling on my sandwich while I wait. After a few minutes, I worry the guide ghost has decided not to follow me. But a few moments later, Laura Tarkington walks to my table and stands in front of me. Her face is carefully neutral. It's only when I give her a smile that she moves closer.

The guide ghost doesn't waver like Terrance Sims, because she's more than a memory. Like Violet, her form is solid—a sign that she has a firm reason to be in the world of the living. If I were to reach out and touch the ghost, her skin would be ice-cold.

She peers over to inspect my sandwich. "Peanut butter and jelly. Always a good choice."

I can hear her voice clearly. As a kid in Boston, I discovered early on that I could hear the voices of the dead. My father always thought I was speaking to imaginary friends until I told him they were actually ghosts—and he didn't believe me. That's when I learned if I wanted to speak with the dead, I needed to do it somewhere away from as many living people as possible.

"I'm sorry about the first time we met," I whisper. "I didn't mean to yell."

"I'm sorry I frightened you, Wednesday."

I'm startled when she calls me by my name. "You know who I am?"

"Everyone seems to know who you are at this school."

"Kind of made that easy on my first day." I give her a wry grin. "I know who you are too—you're Laura Tarkington. You taught language arts here."

The guide ghost's face lights up in pride. "Yes, I decided to return to the school because I like seeing my students."

Some ghosts—especially guides—thrive among the living and go to the places that gave them comfort. Only ghosts with unfinished business are bound to the places they died.

Curiosity spins in my brain, and I venture forth with another question. "Are there other ghosts like you here?"

"No . . . not like before."

Laura Tarkington looks over my head toward the cafeteria doors, surveying the other tables around us. A tingle travels down my spine, and I nervously turn and look around too. But I don't see any other ghosts.

"Maybe they've crossed over," I say.

She looks back down at me. "No, they haven't left. I believe they're hiding."

Coldness creeps into my fingers, but I keep the alarm off my face. Ghosts can use their free will to reveal themselves—even to their own kind. But they also hide when they sense a threat.

Laura Tarkington leans closer. "I'm worried about them. Do you think you can help me find them?"

The bell rings and students rise from the lunch tables. I wrap my half-eaten sandwich and push it into my lunch bag.

"I—I don't know," I stutter as I get up from the table and walk toward the cafeteria doors.

But before I go inside, I look back at the guide ghost. Her flushed-pink face is full of hope.

CHAPTER THIRTEEN

After school, I decide to visit Lincoln at the Beloved Bakery. I don't know if I'm going to help Laura Tarkington yet, so I might as well eat a red velvet cupcake while I think about it.

I walk through the park and instead of going straight toward Noble Avenue to Nana's house, I veer left onto Prince Street and travel the few blocks to where the neighborhood businesses are located. I pass by a hardware shop, a Mexican cantina, a natural-food store, and Nobletown Pizza before I arrive at the Beloved Bakery.

An awning shades a white wicker sofa with red and black throw pillows. A large ceramic bulldog, the university's mascot, crouches beside it. A sign has the cupcakes of the day written in blue chalk, but several have been crossed out—including red velvet. My stomach growls in protest.

When I open the bakery's door, a clanging bell announces my arrival. Inside three people are waiting in line. A brown-skinned girl with a coily puff is working the register.

"Welcome to the Beloved Bakery!" Her voice is full of rehearsed cheer. "Be with you in a moment!"

At one of the small tables, I'm surprised to see Danni-Lynn hunched over a notebook scribbling furiously. An untouched red velvet cupcake is on a plate next to her expensive purse.

It's weird seeing her alone since she's always with Miki, but I walk over and clear my throat to get her attention.

"Oh!" Her light brown cheeks flare pink and she quickly closes the notebook. "Hey, Wednesday."

"Didn't mean to scare you. What were you writing?"

"Nothing," she says quickly before she caves in. "Okay, you're going to think it's silly, but I'm writing *Loveburned* fanfic."

Although I haven't watched any episodes of Danni-Lynn's favorite series or read the *Loveburned* comics, I know about the huge fandom. I haven't read any fanfic either, but I know it's a big deal online.

"I don't think it's silly at all. Do you put your writing up on any of the sites?"

"I use a pen name, but I'm kind of a big deal." Danni-Lynn suppresses a proud smile. "A lot of people like my stories—they're always begging me to write more."

"Maybe you'll be a famous author one day," I tell her.

"Oh, I don't know about all that. I'm just obsessed with *Loveburned*—the characters are so real, and I want to keep their storylines going. Sometimes I can hear their voices in my head, and I write down what they tell me." Danni-Lynn stops talking and her cheeks flush pink again. "I know that sounds strange, but writing *Loveburned* fic makes me feel better."

Danni-Lynn puts the rainbow notebook in her purse. She fidgets in her chair, and we stare awkwardly at each other for a moment. "You want to sit down?"

I glance back at the register and two people are still waiting in line, so I take a seat at the table.

Danni-Lynn leans forward and her pearl necklace clinks against a glass of water. "I don't know if you saw the sign out front, but they're out of red velvet cupcakes. I got the last one."

"It's okay. They still have key lime. Those are good too." I pause. "I kind of know the owner—he's my godfather."

"Oh, I'm officially jealous of you now." Danni-Lynn pouts playfully.

The bell clangs again, and a group of girls enter the bakery. They look like Danni-Lynn—Southern belle types with expensive purses that match their outfits—but I don't recognize any of them from school. The tallest one, a girl with long blond hair and cool blue eyes, smiles and waves at Danni-Lynn. But then she whispers to the other girls, and they all laugh before going to look at the cupcakes in the display case. Danni-Lynn narrows her eyes at them, and my stomach fills with unease.

The group whines loudly about their favorite cupcakes being sold out, and the girl working the register rolls her eyes as they leave the bakery. Outside on the sidewalk, they cluster close as one of them takes out a phone to take group selfies.

The tall blond girl has stayed behind and saunters over to our table. "How you doing, Danni-Lynn? Saw your mama the other day. Told us she went down to Clayburn County to see your daddy."

Danni-Lynn frowns and I think about all the news articles I read about her father. Now I wonder if Tate Porter would get the appeal trial like his lawyer promised at the press conference.

The blond girl looks at me, appraising my blue and gold braids with disapproval. "I don't think we've met. Are you one of Danni-Lynn's *public school* friends?"

Although her voice sounds sweet and nice, the words feel bitter and mean. Before I can say anything, a girl from the group opens the bakery door.

"Audrey, come on!"

Danni-Lynn's face is now pink and blotchy, and I can almost feel the heat of her anger from across the table.

"Time to go, Addie," Danni-Lynn says to the girl. "It would be a shame for history to repeat itself, wouldn't it?"

Audrey's eyes go wide in fear, and she takes two steps backward from our table. Danni-Lynn smirks as the girl leaves the bakery and follows her friends into Nobletown Pizza next door.

"How—how do you know her?"

Danni-Lynn cuts her eyes away from the door and looks at me. "I've known Audrey Abbott all my life. We're first cousins on my mama's side. Me and Daddy have always been outcasts in that family. See, it was cute when Daddy played football while Mama dated him, but it became a real problem when she married him."

Olivia had told me about some of the families in Alton with long histories and university buildings named after them. The ones who drove vintage cars and went to fancy tailgates on North Campus. The ones who gave Nana a hard time when she integrated the neighborhood.

"All those girls go to Alton Academy," Danni-Lynn continues. "That's where I used to go before I got expelled."

My face widens in shock. "You were *expelled*?"

"I got in a fight with Audrey and broke her nose. If you look close at her face, it doesn't look quite right, so it was worth it. Anyway, that happened two years ago. Ancient history."

When Danni-Lynn gives me a bright, vicious smile, I realize underneath her sweet manner is a girl who can take care of herself and won't hesitate to use her fists as an option.

"You know I don't care about all that, right?" I tell her. "*You* didn't do anything wrong."

The light in Danni-Lynn's eyes dims. "Someone told you what happened with my daddy?"

"I read about the trial online," I answer sheepishly. "But I wasn't trying to be nosy, it's just—"

"You don't need to explain," Danni-Lynn interrupts. "It's not a secret. For the record, my daddy made a bad decision, but he's not a bad person."

Suddenly, her eyes fill up with tears, and she startles me when she reaches out to squeeze my hand. "I know he's guilty, and even though Mama claims she's going to find a way to get him out of prison, I know he's not coming home. Not anytime soon."

Danni-Lynn has always been full of charm, so seeing her emotional like this makes my chest ache.

"I'm so, so sorry." I squeeze her hand back.

"It's been hard." Danni-Lynn's voice breaks.

I look up as Lincoln approaches our table. "Everything okay here?"

Danni-Lynn sniffs and smiles at him sweetly. "I'm just devastated you sold out of red velvet cupcakes."

Lincoln glances at Danni-Lynn's plate, and his face softens at her obvious lie. "Hey now, no crying over cupcakes!" He turns to me. "Wednesday, how come you didn't let me know you were out here with a friend?"

"I didn't want to bother you while you were working."

"Please, stop it already." He motions to get the attention of the girl working the register. "Lisa, grab two three-counts for these special ladies."

"You don't have to do this," I protest.

He opens his arms wide in boastful pride. "Whose bakery is this? Yours or mine?"

"Wednesday, don't argue with the owner—not when he wants to give us free cupcakes." Danni-Lynn laughs as the light comes back into her brown eyes.

"I knew I liked this girl." Lincoln smiles at her. "You're one of my regulars. Danielle, right?"

"Danni-Lynn," she corrects him.

"Well, any friend of Wednesday's is a friend of mine."

Lincoln squeezes my shoulder as he heads back to the counter and passes Lisa, who arrives at our table with two turquoise boxes.

"I put two key lime and one birthday cake in each one," she says.

"You can have mine." I push my box toward Danni-Lynn. "Give it to your mother."

"Thank you, Wednesday." She pauses. "You have a good heart."

A surge of warmth rises in my chest—it's the same feeling I got when I first met Miki in Ms. Kimball's class.

I also realize neither one of us has talked about the Dead Club or Violet. I haven't thought about ghosts at all. In this moment sitting at a table in the Beloved Bakery, Danni-Lynn and I are just two girls who are becoming friends.

CHAPTER FOURTEEN

It takes a few more days to get another invitation to the Dead Club. In Ms. Kimball's class, Miki slips me a shiny silver envelope. I'm disappointed it doesn't have any glitter in it, though.

This time when I arrive at Miki's house, I go directly into her backyard and knock on the clubhouse door. Miki quickly answers, smiling wide.

"Hi, Wednesday. Welcome back."

The room looks the same, except silver balloons hover above us. Danni-Lynn is sitting on the sofa and gives me her debutante wave.

Both girls have on the same clothes from school. Miki is wearing her cuffed jeans and a blouse patterned with orange blossoms, but she's pulled her hair out of its French braid and it falls like a black curtain over her shoulders. Danni-Lynn still has on the plaid dress with her trademark pearls, but her curly brown hair is in the same style—sleek with gel and up in a high bun.

At school, we've all stayed friendly, but we don't talk about the Dead Club. In the last few days, I've eaten lunch on the patio waiting to talk with the guide ghost again. But

Laura Tarkington never shows up, which I find strange. Violet also hasn't made another appearance, even though I still keep a vigil at my window at night.

"Are you nervous about taking the oath?" Miki asks.

"No . . . should I be?"

"Don't worry, we're not going to prick your finger for blood," Danni-Lynn assures me. "It's not that dramatic."

"Let's not waste any more time," Miki says. "Do you have any questions before we start?"

When I shake my head, Miki goes to retrieve a wooden box from the nearest bookshelf. When she opens it, she holds up a hardcover of *Wait Till Helen Comes*, but this one has a different cover. A pale hand reaches out from a dark lake. This cover is scarier than the other one.

"It's signed by the author." Miki opens the book to the title page. "See?"

I stare at Mary Downing Hahn's signature. "Fancy."

"Remember when we told you every member has to take the oath on *Helen*?"

I nod as Miki gently places my hand on top of the book.

"The oath is in three parts, so listen carefully. Remember, once you give your word, then it becomes a bond to the club."

I glance down at my hand before looking into Miki's eyes. She's totally serious. This isn't some silly game to her.

"Are you sure you're ready, Wednesday?" Danni-Lynn asks from the sofa. "The club oath is nothing to mess with at all."

"Yeah, I understand."

Danni-Lynn seems satisfied at my answer and gives her approval to start the ceremony.

Miki clears her throat. "Wednesday Thomas, do you solemnly swear to keep the secrets of the dead, to hold the dead in the highest honor, and to protect the dead from the living?"

I press my lips tight to disguise my surprise. I wasn't expecting this kind of oath. In the awkward silence that follows, Miki moves closer to me.

"Remember, your word is a bond to the club. If you're not sure you can fulfill this first part, we can just stop now."

My family has always honored the dead, so this was something I already believed. "I swear," I say.

Danni-Lynn opens a notebook. When she's finished writing, she nods again at Miki to continue with the second part of the oath.

Miki locks eyes with me again. "Wednesday Thomas, do you solemnly swear to keep the existence of the Dead Club secret, to never disclose its members, and to never speak of it at school?"

I don't hesitate with my answer this time. "I swear."

Danni-Lynn records my response in the notebook again, and then Miki takes a long breath before she states the final part of the oath.

"Wednesday Thomas, do you solemnly swear to disclose what the dead tell you, to never lie about what the dead reveal, and to be honest about your contact with the dead?"

This time I hesitate, because the last part of the club oath seems to be directed specifically to me as a medium.

"You have to answer truthfully to all three parts," Danni-Lynn tells me. "If you can't then you won't fulfill the oath, and you won't be a full member."

"Do you need me to repeat the third part for you, Wednesday?" Miki asks.

"No, I—" I stop to take a deep breath. "I swear."

After scribbling in the notebook again, Danni-Lynn claps happily. Miki removes my hand from the book.

"Congratulations!" she says. "I formally pronounce Wednesday Thomas an official member of the Dead Club."

We celebrate with cookies and punch, but it doesn't take long before Miki announces the start of official Dead Club business.

Danni-Lynn opens the club notebook, and I push my weight deeper into the beanbag chair and wait in anticipation.

Miki moves to the edge of the sofa. "Before we talk about Violet, we need to share some details about the club. I'm the president and oath keeper. Danni-Lynn is the secretary and club historian."

"Violet was the Dead Club's founder," Danni-Lynn tells me. "She's the one who invited us to become members."

"I took over as president when Violet died," Miki says softly.

Danni-Lynn gently pats Miki's knee. "A lot of people

thought Violet was weird, but I don't fault her for that. She grew up across the street from a haunted house, so she was bound to be a little touched. And let me tell you, Violet *loved* ghosts. When I got expelled and transferred to Noble, she was one of the few people at school who were nice to me. Listening to her spooky stories was better than dealing with my own life—especially after my daddy's trial. By the time she brought me into the club, I was already kind of hooked on ghosts too."

I think of the photo of Violet on her birthday. She'd been so happy with her friends. At that time, I didn't know the girls were members of a secret club who wanted to communicate with the dead.

"It was hard for us when Violet died," Miki says.

I didn't know much about bacterial meningitis before my research for Violet, but I learned the infection is contagious and can spread like the flu or strep throat. Although most people can recover, others can die within a few hours or days. That's what happened to Violet—after she got sick, it didn't take long for her to pass away.

"It's hard to lose someone so quickly and without warning," I say quietly.

"It was like a nightmare, except we never woke up." Miki looks away as she wrings her hands. "Then last Halloween, we saw her ghost."

Most ghosts can reveal themselves between sunset and sunrise on Halloween. No one in my family knows the reason why this happens—but on this sacred night, the dead like to mingle with the living. Some resolve unfinished business while others reconnect with loved ones.

"True believers can see the dead on Halloween," I tell Miki. "What did Violet say? Did she ask you for help?"

The girls exchange looks for a moment. Even though I'm an official club member now, it seems they're still being careful about what they reveal to me.

Danni-Lynn closes the club notebook. "At the meet and greet, you asked us if there were other members. Well, you should know there's one other person."

I don't wait for Danni-Lynn to tell me who it is because I already know. "Is it Alexa Scott?"

Miki frowns at me. "Did she say something to you?"

"No—not exactly."

"What do you mean?" Miki's voice raises an octave. "Did Alexa mention the club to you or not? Is that why you were avoiding me at school?"

"No, she never mentioned the club to me," I quickly answer. "But she—she did tell me to stay away from both of you."

Miki jumps up from the sofa and grabs her phone off the table. Her thumbs jab angrily at the screen. Danni-Lynn releases a weary sigh.

"Who's she texting?"

"Alexa," Danni-Lynn answers.

"So Alexa *is* a member of this club?"

Danni-Lynn shrugs. "She took the oath."

"She's not answering my texts!" Miki complains as she

returns to the sofa and flops, defeated, into the cushions. "Wednesday, are you sure Alexa didn't say *anything* else to you?"

"She barely talks to me at school, but I think she knows I can see ghosts. On my first day, she kind of overheard me say the school was haunted, and she didn't seem surprised."

Miki lets out a petty laugh, which confuses me even more. "Oh, she knows *all* about the ghosts at school. She's the one who told us about them."

The girls stare as the revelation slowly comes to me. The words that form on my tongue surprise me at first, but then I think back on everything that's happened. My interactions with Alexa, and her advice to keep a low profile and act normal. It all makes sense now.

"Alexa can see the dead," I whisper.

CHAPTER FIFTEEN

Both girls continue to stare at me, but Miki breaks the spell by grabbing her phone to check her texts. Danni-Lynn snatches it away before Miki can send another message. Sinking into the sofa pillows, Miki doesn't even protest—she actually looks relieved.

"Yes, Alexa can see ghosts. Just like you. She was the first medium for the Dead Club," Danni-Lynn confirms.

"Why isn't she the club's medium now?" I ask.

"After Violet died, she stopped coming to the meetings," Danni-Lynn tells me. "She made it clear that she didn't want to be a member anymore."

"Alexa doesn't want to help us." Miki's face is full of intense conviction. "She doesn't *care*."

Maybe Alexa couldn't share her sadness with Miki and Danni-Lynn. The burden of death can be hard on the living, and grief can take many forms. Some people show their devastation openly while others shut down their emotions. Maybe Violet's death was so painful that Alexa didn't want to be around other people who loved her too. But she was the club's medium, and with her gift, she had the ability to get closure with Violet's ghost. If Alexa knew Violet was still on this physical plane, why didn't she want to communicate with her?

"We've tried to contact Violet in a lot of different ways," Danni-Lynn says. "We've held séances, tried a Ouija board, went out on full moons during witching hours—nothing has worked."

"You can't make the dead speak to you—not if they don't want to. I don't even have that power," I say.

"We were planning to contact Violet on Halloween again," Miki tells me. "But then you moved into the Callahan House and you're Josephine Marlow's blood relative. I don't believe in coincidences, so this is fate. Wednesday, you were meant to help us."

My face flushes as Miki beams at me. It's the same look she gave me after I raced out of the cafeteria on my first day of school.

A bright flame wavers in my brain. Without Alexa, the Dead Club hasn't been able to contact Violet. Am I just a replacement? What happens after I help them? I shift my weight in the beanbag chair and push the troubling thoughts away.

Danni-Lynn opens the club notebook. "How many times have you seen Violet?"

"Twice. But the first time, I didn't realize she was a ghost—that can happen with the newly dead."

I decide not to share my initial fear of Violet, because now I know it was my experience with the wicked ghost in Arizona that made me afraid of her.

The soft scribble of Danni-Lynn's pen on paper is the

only noise in the room. Miki inches to the edge of the sofa and nods eagerly for me to continue.

"When I saw Violet the second time, I offered to help her find out what happened to her parents. She didn't seem to remember much about her life."

Danni-Lynn stops writing and looks up. "Can ghosts forget who they are?"

"I've helped a lot of ghosts remember by doing research for them," I answer. "The information I give them is usually enough to help them cross over."

The girls give each other another knowing look, and I wonder if there's something else they haven't told me yet.

"Where did you see Violet on Halloween?" I ask.

"We were walking back to my house from the Fall Festival in the park," Miki says. "Violet was sitting on her porch. It—it was like she was waiting for us."

"Did she recognize who you were?" I ask.

Miki slowly nods. "She knew us."

"She wanted us to contact the Callahan ghost," Danni-Lynn says.

I push my weight deeper into the beanbag chair. Why would Violet need to speak to Caleb Callahan? The dead only needed help communicating with the living.

"That doesn't make sense," I say. "Did Violet say why she wanted to talk with Caleb?"

"To be honest, we were kind of freaked out about seeing her." Danni-Lynn visibly shivers. "But we both clearly heard her say that to us."

"Then she just . . . disappeared." Miki hands are now gripped on her knees. "She didn't ask . . . she didn't even ask if we missed her."

"After Miki told Alexa what happened, she still wouldn't help us." Danni-Lynn frowns as she touches her pearl necklace.

"But Violet was her friend too. Maybe I can talk to her—"

"We don't *need* Alexa," Miki interrupts me. "You're the club's medium now. You *live* in the Callahan House."

"Have you seen Caleb?" Danni-Lynn asks.

"No, I haven't," I tell her. "Remember, I can't make the dead speak to me."

"Violet wanted us to contact Caleb, and you're our best hope to do that," Miki says.

Violet hadn't mentioned the Callahan ghost to me. What had changed since last Halloween when she appeared to Miki and Danni-Lynn?

"I don't know if Caleb will speak to me," I tell them. "But I can try to contact him."

After my first official club meeting, I walk slowly through the neighborhood back to Nana's house. Some neighbors have put fall wreaths or skeletons on their doors. Others have decorated porches with stacks of hay, pumpkins, and ceramic pots filled with colorful mums. Scarecrows and tombstones appear in a few yards—these neighbors seem eager to embrace the Halloween season, but fall hasn't arrived in Georgia yet. The trees haven't changed color, and the sidewalks are bare of crunchy leaves. The humidity hangs heavy in the air, making my braids feel sticky on my neck.

Despite the warm afternoon, I feel a slight chill on my skin when I think about Violet.

I offered to find information about her parents, which made sense—most ghosts want to know what happened to their loved ones before they move on. But Violet had asked her friends to contact Caleb Callahan. A boy who died over seventy-five years ago. Violet didn't know him in life, so why did she want to contact him in death?

When I arrive at Nana's house, I lean against the gate and stare across the street. It doesn't matter if I want Violet to answer my questions. I can't make her tell me why she wants to speak to the Callahan ghost.

I wait for a few more moments, willing the ghost of Violet Delgado to appear on her porch. Disappointment brews in my chest when she doesn't.

CHAPTER SIXTEEN

When I enter the house, the faint thumping of music tells me Olivia is up in the turret working. I peek in the library, and although Jasmine isn't there, she's left signs of her earlier presence. An empty glass sits on a coaster next to a mess of papers on the mahogany desk. She's also added more textbooks to the bookshelves.

The savory tang of tomatoes and onions leads my nose into the kitchen. In the oven, a chicken tortilla casserole bubbles in a glass dish. But I forget about my favorite meal when the temperature in the kitchen dramatically drops. A flicker of movement catches the corner of my eye. Then the back hallway door creaks open, and Olivia's music grows louder.

I wait a few heartbeats before I walk to the door. It creaks loudly again as I open it wider. The air is colder, but I don't see anything in the murky darkness.

I let out a startled yelp when the doorbell rings—it's the first time I've heard it since moving into the house. I return my gaze to the gloomy back stairs, but the Callahan ghost hasn't appeared. When the regal chord chimes again, I go through the kitchen to the main entryway. The leaded glass distorts the person outside into broad geometric shapes.

When I open the door, Alexa is standing on the porch. She's changed out of her school clothes and is wearing shorts and a loose T-shirt. Alexa's hair is pulled away from her face with a sports headband. Wary eyes and a tight frown make it clear she isn't happy to see me.

"Miki has been sending me texts for the last hour," Alexa says. "I left practice early to come talk to you."

I study her face to find any signs of her gift, but I already know there isn't a way to tell if someone can see the dead.

"Do you want to hear what I have to say?" she asks.

"Yes, sorry. Come in."

I guide her into the den, but she doesn't sit on the sofa. She remains standing and crosses her arms like she's cold. The temperature hasn't changed in the den, but I wonder if she can sense the Callahan ghost in the house.

"I'm assuming Miki and Danni-Lynn told you everything about me," she says. "Even though I told you to stay away from them."

"Why didn't you just tell me yourself?"

Alexa looks away and doesn't respond. Her face contorts into a kind of inner turmoil, as if she's struggling to decide what to reveal. "I didn't want to be wrong about you, so I needed to be careful."

When I lived in Boston, I was this way too. Cautious about everything. I never wanted anyone to know what I could do. It was safer. I saw how my classmates treated others who were different. It was easier for me to disappear into the background and not bring attention to myself. But Alexa wasn't alone like me. She had Violet, Miki, and Danni-Lynn. She was the Dead Club's medium.

The tension in her face disappears, and Alexa uncrosses her arms. We stare at each for a moment. Maybe now she's looking for any signs in me—some external clue that reveals we're the same.

"Why are you willing to talk to me now?" I ask.

Alexa sharply inhales in aggravation. "I don't know what Miki has told you, but you need to leave Violet alone."

"But—"

"She's dangerous, Wednesday."

Alexa's mouth tightens into a scowl, and I can tell she's serious. My brain fills up with an electric static—a buzzing noise of alarm.

I quickly recall my interactions with Violet. The ghost didn't show any signs of being dangerous.

Alexa's face changes again—a brief glimpse of fear before the irritation replaces it. The static in my brain gets louder.

"Did Miki tell you what happened to me last Halloween?" she asks.

"What happened to you?" I whisper. "Did Violet—did she try to hurt you?"

Alexa nods but doesn't speak. Her eyes glaze over like she's revisiting a haunting ordeal. Her shoulders slump, and she slowly sits on the sofa as if to recover from the experience all over again. I wonder if her brain feels like a small hurricane is swirling or if her heart is racing. I wonder if her legs itch to run.

My throat turns dry, and I push away my own dark memories, forcing myself back into the present moment.

When Alexa's storm passes, her eyes are clear and determined. She's fully back from the memory of that night.

"I came here to warn you," she tells me. "Stay away from Violet and leave that club alone."

We both turn at the loud creak at the top of the staircase that's quickly followed by the sound of soft footfalls, and Olivia appears in a paint-splotched jumper.

"I thought I heard the doorbell," she says.

Alexa quickly adjusts her face and gives Olivia a polite smile. I wonder how much of the conversation Olivia has heard. She returns Alexa's smile and seems unaware of the tension in the room.

"This is Alexa Scott," I say. "She goes to Noble too."

"Oh, it's so nice to meet one of Wednesday's friends." Olivia's smile grows wider.

Alexa's own smile falters. "I came by to see Wednesday for a quick visit, but I need to go back to the school. My mom usually picks me up after volleyball practice."

Olivia glances at both of us. I wonder if she can tell we aren't friends at all. "That's too bad, I was going to invite you to dinner. Maybe another time?"

"Uh, sure," Alexa says.

After a few seconds of awkward silence, Olivia comes over and squeezes my shoulder as if trying to give me some kind of support. "I'm going to go check on the casserole. Nice meeting you, Alexa."

When Olivia heads to the kitchen, Alexa's fake smile disappears. She marches to the front door, and I quickly follow her. I still have so many other things I want to ask her. How did she stop the wicked ghost from devouring her? How did she escape from the danger? Did she use her own version of a Lodestar—did she follow a guiding light to safety? But Alexa's face is closed off as she leaves the house.

I rush out on the porch and grab her hand, a last-ditch effort to get her to say something to me. Alexa's face is so full of fear, and I'm not sure if it's for her or for me.

When I let go of her hand, she doesn't say a word. She turns and walks to the gate. Not once does she look back at me.

The Callahan House, September 21, 1999

On Noble Avenue, where the old Victorian still stood, Olivia Moore waited on the porch.

She hoped the boy from her third-grade class would meet her so that she could prove the house was haunted. Everyone at her new school knew about the Callahan family and their tragic deaths. Some were curious and asked about the spirits, while others were rude and called her a witch.

Since coming to Alton, Olivia quickly learned that speaking with the dead made her a target of both fascination and ridicule.

But one of the dead had saved Olivia's life.

When the fire had swiftly taken her parents, a girl with a burned face led Olivia through the smoke to safety.

A hollow pang returned to Olivia's chest, and she quickly pushed the memory away. She wasn't going to think about the fire or her parents.

From the porch, she stared at a car parked in front of the house. Olivia's grandmother received many guests seeking answers from spirits, and these out-of-town patrons usually left with the answers they needed. The local ones were more discreet. They parked several blocks away and entered through the sunporch to avoid being seen at the front door.

It had been this way since Josephine Marlow purchased the house in 1966. Back in those days, one of her white patrons had to secure the deed. Only five years earlier, the university had admitted their first Black students. When Olivia's grandmother first integrated the neighborhood, there were several angry outbursts from the neighbors, but eventually the loudest ones quietly became Josephine's patrons.

When Olivia saw the dark-skinned boy loping down Noble Avenue, she scrambled to meet him at the gate.

"I didn't think you were coming," she said, trying to hide her relief at the boy's arrival.

"I keep my word," the boy said.

Lincoln Reed had heard the rumors all his life. At his family's bakery, his mother and aunts whispered about the old woman's haunted house. Lincoln wanted to see for himself if the stories about the Callahan ghost were true.

"You're not scared?" Olivia asked.

Lincoln shook his head as Olivia opened the gate to let him in the yard. He followed her until she reached the porch.

"The spirit in the house isn't dangerous." Olivia paused, biting her lip. "But you might not be able to see him."

When doubt appeared on the boy's face, Olivia's heart sank. Lincoln wanted proof, but she knew he couldn't see the dead like she could. Before she could convince him that the spirit in the house was indeed real, the front door opened, and Josephine Marlow stood tall in the entryway.

Josephine's coily silver hair was in its usual bun, and she wore one of the black dresses she reserved for patron visits. Her dark brown skin was mostly unlined, defying her age of seventy-five years. She stared hard at the boy in her yard.

"Tell this boy he needs to leave, Olivia."

Olivia's eyes widened at her grandmother's sharp tone, but she quickly turned to Lincoln. "Maybe you can visit another time?"

Lincoln didn't bother to answer and stumbled through the yard to the gate. He gave Olivia one last look before he ran down the sidewalk. It would take the boy several years to gather up his courage to visit Olivia again.

Josephine pulled her granddaughter into the house, steering her away from the den.

"A woman is here with her daughter." Her voice remained low and firm. "I believe a wicked spirit has taken up with the little girl."

A rush of dread pulsed through Olivia as she glanced at the closed sliding doors to the den. Cunning and ruthless, wicked spirits feasted on living souls and stole faces of the dead. Olivia had faith that her Lodestar could provide protection if she was ever attacked, but now that a wicked spirit was in her grandmother's house, she trembled in fright.

"No need for you to worry, baby," her grandmother reassured her. "You know who dwells in this house."

Olivia had seen the frail spirit with sad eyes. For over fifty years, Caleb Callahan had remained a bound spirit in the house. Even after her grandmother told Olivia about Caleb's unique power, she doubted the pale redheaded boy could conquer a wicked spirit.

"Go upstairs to your room," her grandmother told her. "Stay there until I come for you."

Josephine waited until her granddaughter raced up the staircase and closed the door to her room. She didn't believe that her granddaughter was ready to witness a banishment. At least not yet. But Olivia would never get another opportunity to witness a wicked spirit dispelled from a living body.

Smoothing out her black dress, Josephine walked toward the closed sliding doors. When she entered the den, the woman and her daughter waited on the sofa. The little girl watched Josephine with mild curiosity. Although no cold air hovered in the room, Josephine could sense the unnatural chill on the little girl's skin, a warning that the wicked spirit was curled tight around her heart.

When Caleb appeared in the den, the little girl's curiosity turned to suspicion. Her mother couldn't see the small boy. He was only a few years older than her daughter, wearing striped pajamas and the bruises of death around his neck.

Caleb stared at the little girl, and the anger rumbled in him when she showed him her teeth instead of a smile. He remembered a similar smile, although he'd forgotten how long ago that had been. Time had no meaning to him now, but he knew what lurked inside the child sitting on the sofa. It was the same kind of dead thing that had entered his room on that warm November night.

Only after the woman felt the freezing cold did her eyes turn to Josephine in alarm. Her daughter had explained what she saw when the temperature dropped, so the woman knew a dead person was in the room with them.

"Follow my directions," Josephine quickly told her. "We're going to have to hold your daughter down. No matter what happens or what she says, don't let go. Do you understand me?"

Upstairs, Olivia sat on the bed and let her shoulders release their tension. The house remained silent, and the exhausting fear faded in her body. She lay down on the thick comforter, placing a hand over her heart.

She bolted up at the bloodcurdling scream that pierced the walls. Afraid to move, Olivia waited for the next horrific scream, but it never came. Only silence.

The top step of the staircase creaked loudly, and Olivia rose from the bed, wary about who was approaching her room. She wasn't sure if it would be her grandmother or the wicked spirit cloaked in her body.

At the sound of a soft tap, Olivia slowly walked to the door, but she didn't open it. After another soft tap, a voice spoke.

"You can open this door now," her grandmother said.

Olivia placed a trembling hand over the crystal doorknob. "Is the wicked spirit gone?"

"Please open the door, baby."

Olivia let out a trembling breath. A wicked spirit wouldn't knock, nor would it ask to enter her room.

When she opened the door, her grandmother was on the other side. Some of her silver hair had escaped from her bun, but otherwise she looked unharmed. The cold didn't prick Olivia's skin with any warnings. Her Lodestar remained dormant; no evil wrapped around her grandmother's heart.

Downstairs, Olivia searched for any signs of the wicked spirit's banishment. It wasn't until she entered the den that she found any evidence. A large blot, black as ink, marred the hardwood floor. By nightfall, the stain would disappear without a trace, and Olivia would learn how the wicked spirit came to its demise.

On the sofa, the woman sipped dark liquor from a stout glass, and Olivia's nose twitched from the strong aroma of the aged bourbon. The woman's blanched face was sweaty, and dark hair stuck to her forehead. Her daughter had sat up, but the little girl's eyes were vacant and her mouth hung slightly open.

At first, Olivia wondered if it had been the woman she'd heard upstairs, but now she had an answer: the little girl had been the one who'd screamed.

"Cecily should be fine now," Olivia's grandmother told the woman. "Take her back home and let her rest."

Although the room was humid and warm, the woman's haunted face made Olivia cautious. The little girl stared at the inky stain on the floor. As the spot continued to shrink, her eyes grew more alert with awareness.

"The abomination that was in my daughter—it can't come back, right?" the woman asked Josephine.

"The wicked spirit is gone, but I can't promise you that another one won't find her," Josephine answered truthfully. "It's rare, but it happens."

Over the years Josephine had learned that Lodestars were not common among those who could see the dead. Although she'd tried to teach others how to access the guiding light inside them, no time or practice had ever conjured any success. Josephine now understood Lodestars were a rare bloodline blessing.

The woman's hand shook as she drained the rest of the bourbon. The little girl slowly stopped looking at the floor and focused her stare on Olivia.

"Are you like me?" she asked.

The odd gaze on the little girl's face made Olivia nervous. She moved closer to her grandmother and remained silent.

"I used to like seeing dead people," the little girl told Olivia sadly. "They were my friends, but I don't like them anymore. I want them to go away."

When the woman rose from the sofa, she took her daughter's hand. Olivia followed her grandmother, and they escorted the patrons to the front door. Olivia noticed the little girl's eyes were now clear, but they weren't peaceful.

"Miss Josephine, there are no words to explain how grateful I am to you," the woman said solemnly.

"I try to do what I can," Josephine told her. "But I do hope this is the last time you come to this house."

The woman never returned to the old Victorian on Noble Avenue, and no other wicked spirit would possess her daughter. When Cecily Thorne turned fourteen, she lost her gift to see the dead, but the memory of this day would haunt her for the rest of her life.

CHAPTER SEVENTEEN

I go up to my room and sit at my desk stewing in a mix of fear and confusion.

Miki hadn't shared the *real* reason Alexa stopped being the club's medium. Did Danni-Lynn know about this too? I fidget with the possibility. I took the oath and gave my word to be truthful. Now it seemed the club's president hadn't shared the whole truth with me.

I feel queasy. Would Miki put me in harm's way? Did she care about my safety? Did she even consider me a friend?

My mind drifts back to what Miki told me. *Alexa doesn't want to help us. She doesn't care.*

Alexa didn't stop being the club's medium because she didn't care—Alexa was afraid. If Miki knew this, then she was the one who didn't care.

My breath hitches with more spiraling thoughts, and I push them away because I don't want to believe them. Miki has been sincerely nice to me, and I can't dismiss the genuine warmth of friendship I felt with her—those moments were real.

I've seen how Violet's death has affected Miki. I know the effect grief can have on the living—the emotional wounds and the lingering regret. She kept the club going because she wanted to help Violet.

But I've also seen the fear in Alexa's eyes. From my own experience, I know she's telling the truth. More than likely, I encountered the same wicked ghost with Violet's stolen face.

I reach for my phone. The last text I received from Miki was a row of green heart emojis. I type and then delete angry words, and a deep anxiety fills my body at the thought of confronting her. After my anger subsides, I send a message.

Wednesday: alexa just left my house. why didn't you tell me the truth about what happened to her?

Typing bubbles immediately appear, and my heart speeds up as I wait for Miki to respond. My brain buzzes with all the possible things she could say. Maybe she'll confess about keeping the truth from me.

The typing bubbles disappear, and I wait for them to pop back up on the phone's screen. When they never do, I dial Miki's number, but it goes directly to voicemail.

She doesn't want to talk to me.

I try to enjoy my favorite meal, but I can barely taste it. Alexa's words burn inside me like the desert sun.

Stay away from Violet and leave that club alone.

I sit cross-legged on the den's rug in front of the low table, pushing food around with my fork. Olivia is perched on the sofa across from me, and the glass dish of our dinner lies between us on an oven mitt. We haven't officially used the dining room properly yet—the old habits of eating in the RV are still with us.

Olivia cuts another square of the chicken tortilla casserole and steam rises as she transfers it to her plate.

"I'm glad you're making lots of friends, Wednesday."

Alexa is far from being one of my friends, but I don't correct Olivia. Instead I listen to her talk about her latest sheet metal designs.

I glance down at my phone. The screen remains dark. No notifications. Miki hasn't called or texted me.

Although Olivia notices my distraction, she doesn't press me for details until we're washing dishes in the kitchen.

"Something on your mind, Wednesday?" she asks.

"Are you sure you haven't met anyone else who can see ghosts?"

Olivia rinses a plate before she answers. "I've always told you other people like us can see spirits. Our family isn't the only one."

Alexa didn't share anything about her family. I don't know which parent gave her the gift to see the dead or how many ghosts she's helped in Alton.

Olivia hands me a plate to dry. "Growing up, it would have been nice to have someone to talk to when I had my gift—someone my age. Link didn't really understand it, but at least he believed me."

Alexa knew I was like her. She's known from the beginning, and she tried to help me in her own way.

After we put the dishes into the cabinets, Olivia gives me a kiss on my cheek, and then walks toward the back stairs.

"Olivia, I need to tell you something."

She turns around, and her face is full of interest. "Is it about the girl who came to visit today? Alexa?"

"How did you—" I pause. "You heard what she said to me, didn't you? You already know she can see ghosts."

Olivia leans against the kitchen island. "Are you going to tell me what's going on?"

"I've sort of agreed to be a medium for some girls," I say. "They have a secret club."

"A secret club?" Olivia raises her eyebrows. "Are these the same girls you've been hanging out with after school?"

I nod slowly. "They were friends with Violet. The girl who lived across the street—the ghost I told you about."

Olivia's eyes turn soft. "Wednesday, I'm sure these girls have good intentions, but you can't promise them anything. Spirits have free will."

"I know," I say. "Alexa was their first medium. But she quit because she found out Violet is a wicked ghost, and I think the club's president already knew that and—"

Olivia holds up her hand to stop me from speaking any further. "Okay, this is where I need you to start from the beginning."

I take a deep breath and tell her everything. Alexa's advice and her warnings. The invitation to the Dead Club and taking the oath. Olivia doesn't interrupt me. After I'm done, she remains quiet.

When she comes to hug me, I burrow my face deep into her neck before she steps back and adjusts my braids over my shoulder.

"Do you think Violet could be . . . wicked?"

Olivia regards me closely. Her eyes are clear and calm. Despite what I've shared with her, she doesn't seem alarmed.

"Nothing wicked can hurt you now, Wednesday. Not anymore."

"But if a wicked ghost is using Violet's face to trick me—"

"You're safe, I promise." Olivia takes my hand and squeezes it. "As long as you're in this house, nothing will harm you."

"I—I don't understand," I say. "I thought my Lodestar kept me safe."

Olivia puts my hand over her heart. "Wednesday, wicked spirits don't want to possess your body—they want to possess your *life*. They want to *replace* you. This is how they can live several lifetimes on this plane. I couldn't take the risk of that happening to you. I know you have your Lodestar for protection, but I wanted to bring you back to this house so I could be sure you would be safe."

When I look into Olivia's eyes, I see the truth of her words, and a revelation lights up a tiny spark in my brain.

"It's the Callahan ghost, isn't it?" I whisper. "He's the reason this house is safe."

Olivia squeezes my hand again. "When I was first moved here, a woman brought her daughter to Nana. There was . . . a wicked spirit inside her. Nana made me go upstairs, so I didn't see what happened, but I heard the little girl's scream."

"What happened to the wicked ghost?"

"Caleb banished it," she tells me.

I blink. "How is that possible?"

"Caleb is another type of rare spirit—a banisher. A wicked spirit possessed his father and killed Caleb and his family. In death, Caleb devoured the wicked spirit and banished it to the spirit realm."

I let Olivia's words sink into me. "So Caleb can banish wicked ghosts from this plane?"

Olivia nods. "When Caleb told Nana what happened the night he died, she knew it was his unresolved anger that kept him bound to this house. Over the years, he worked with her to banish other wicked spirits. Caleb is the reason why nothing can hurt you in this house."

"Why didn't you tell me this before?"

"You had already been through so much and I thought you would lose your gift soon." Olivia's eyes fill with tears. "I should have told you when I realized you could still see spirits, so you wouldn't be afraid. I'm so sorry."

Olivia hugs me tight again, and the buzzing in my brain disappears. For the first time since that night in Arizona, I don't feel the nervous energy or panic in my chest. Nana's house is a place of protection, and the Callahan ghost who dwells here is its shield.

"Thank you for telling me about Caleb," I finally say.

"Wednesday, listen to me. If a wicked spirit enters this house—in a stolen form or in a possessed body—Caleb will banish it. I can promise you that."

CHAPTER EIGHTEEN

The next morning, I search for Miki in the hallways, but I don't find her—she's avoiding me.

I arrive early to Ms. Kimball's class, but when the late bell rings, she doesn't show up. This is when I realize Miki hasn't come to school at all.

In the cafeteria, Danni-Lynn sits alone at a high-top table. She's wearing another one of her ruffled blouses and tailored pants. Her hair isn't in a sleek bun today, and her curly brown hair surrounds her head like a halo. With my Grand Canyon T-shirt, jeans, and blue and gold braids, I look like her total opposite. We're two girls who seem like they have nothing in common—at least from our appearances. When Danni-Lynn sees me, she gives a dainty wave and grins wide.

Since the cafeteria disaster with the guide ghost, everyone has already forgotten about me. I'm still the new girl from Las Vegas, but they don't whisper about me anymore.

I do catch Alexa staring at me. When we lock eyes, she frowns at me. A twinge of disappointment shifts in my chest. I've always wanted to meet someone else who could speak to the dead. I want to tell her about Caleb Callahan. I want to let her know Nana's haunted house is a safe haven. But Alexa doesn't want anything to do with me, and I'm not sure if it's worth trying to convince her otherwise.

I sit across from Danni-Lynn. "Do you know where Miki is today?"

"She called me this morning and told me she wasn't feeling well. Knowing Miki, she probably didn't study for her math test."

I pull out my lunch bag. "Is that all she told you?"

Danni-Lynn purses her lips as she studies me and then widens her eyes. "Did y'all have a fight?"

"Not exactly." I unwrap my sandwich.

Danni-Lynn narrows her eyes in suspicion. "What did Miki do?"

I fidget in my seat and glance at Alexa's table. Violet kept the club and its members a secret. It's the reason none of Alexa's friends know she can see ghosts. Miki and Danni-Lynn kept their oaths. Neither one shared anything with me until I became a full member. Miki never told me or even hinted that Alexa was like me. Not telling her secret showed integrity and character, which made Miki's lie even more confusing.

"We can't talk about it here," I tell Danni-Lynn. "It's club business."

Danni-Lynn's face turns serious. "Understood, but I'll have to put this on the agenda for our next meeting. We can't have discord in the club."

I want to ask her if she knows the truth about Alexa, but I decide to respect the oath too.

"Well, since we can't talk about *that* . . ." Danni-Lynn gives me a sly smirk, as if she's about to share some juicy gossip. "Did you hear Leo Stacks walked off the set of *Loveburned*? They're in the middle of filming the final season! The fans are up in arms, and it's breaking my heart. Nobody else can play his character! What is Leo *thinking*?"

My eyes shift to Laura Tarkington as she enters the cafeteria. It's the first time she's appeared since I talked with her on the patio. The guide ghost holds her yellow peacoat tight around her waist. Her flushed pink face looks confused as she moves slowly around the room. She doesn't stop at any tables. Instead, she leans close to the wall and puts her hands to her ears as if the noise bothers her.

Danni-Lynn's voice fades out as I watch the guide ghost leaning against the wall. Laura Tarkington removes her hands from her ears and scans the room. But when she looks at me, her eyes fill with terror, and she bolts out the cafeteria through the patio doors.

"Wednesday," Danni-Lynn repeats my name. "Is something wrong?"

I stand up from the high-top table. "I need to go out to the patio."

Danni-Lynn's face fills up with instant understanding, and she lets me go without any further questions.

When I get outside, there's no sign of the guide ghost. I go to the table in the far corner and sweep off fallen leaves. I slowly eat my sandwich as I wait, but Laura Tarkington never makes an appearance.

• • •

After school, I stand in the empty hallway. When Terrance Sims appears, I let his frosty presence brush against my skin. His luminous face is so full of joy, and the ghost's happiness soothes me. He's only a memory—a wavering presence. Then I think about Laura Tarkington and her fearful face. A burst of distress fills my chest, but I push it away.

"Wednesday," Danni-Lynn's voice comes from behind me.

When I turn, she's squinting and shivering. Although Danni-Lynn can't see the ghost in the green windbreaker, she can feel the chill of him in the air.

"What does he look like?" she whispers.

"Short. Brown skin. Looks young for his age," I tell her. "But he's not really here. It's a memory more than anything."

Danni-Lynn tries to see the ghost for a few more moments before she gives up and opens her bag. "I need to give you something."

I'm confused when she hands me a stack of worksheets and notes. "What's this?"

"Miki's homework assignments. She asked me to get them for her since she's 'not feeling well,'" Danni-Lynn says as she uses her fingers to quote Miki's excuse for not coming to school. "There's a take-home math test in there too, so make sure she does that first."

"Why are you giving this stuff to me?"

"I can't keep my fanfic readers waiting, especially with all this Leo Stacks drama! I've got to get my next *Love-*

burned story finished and posted today." Danni-Lynn gives me a sly, sweet smile. "Also you and Miki need to work out this little spat. You shouldn't wait until the next club meeting."

"I don't think she wants to talk to me. She made that very clear yesterday." I frown. "And I'm not sure I want to talk to her either."

Danni-Lynn shrugs. "Okay, then leave her stuff on the porch."

I bite my lip. I'll have to talk to Miki sooner than later. But I'm not sure what to say to her yet. A bit of anger still festers inside me.

I sigh as I put Miki's homework in my backpack. "Fine. Are you happy now?"

"Overjoyed," Danni-Lynn drawls as she hooks her arm in mine.

When we walk out to the courtyard, the afternoon light is weaker and the breeze has a nip in the air that cuts through my T-shirt. Maybe fall has finally arrived in Alton.

"Hey, do you think your godfather would give me a Beloved Bakery discount?" Danni-Lynn asks.

Her question catches me off guard, and I let out a surprised laugh. "I don't know. You could ask him."

"With all the red velvet cupcakes I eat, I practically keep his business open," she says. "I'll just mention your name in case he forgot we're friends."

Danni-Lynn holds tight to my arm as we journey through the park, but she lets go once we get to Noble

Avenue. It's time for us to part ways. Danni-Lynn needs to write her fanfic at the Beloved Bakery, and I need to confront Miki at her house.

Danni-Lynn walks toward Prince Street, but after a few paces, she turns around. "Make sure to tell Miki I hope she feels better soon!"

CHAPTER NINETEEN

I take a deep breath and travel up the cobblestone walkway to Miki's house. An elderly man wearing a red tracksuit greets me at the door. Gray hair swoops over the top of his thick, round glasses, but he brushes it away and gives me a warm smile.

"Hello, is Miki home?"

He nods, and I hear Miki's faint voice from inside the house. "Ojiichan, Danni-chan desu ka?"

"Hai, kanojo desu!" the elderly man yells over his shoulder.

He invites me to come inside and points to a row of shoes lined up in the foyer. I take off my sneakers as he slowly shuffles down the hallway.

In the family room, a cable news show is muted on the TV. Plants and flowers are everywhere, and the house smells like fresh linen and green leaves.

A happy bark is quickly followed by clinks of metal tags. In a lopsided scurry, a shaggy black dog approaches me and immediately starts licking my socks. It's the same dog I saw in the window on my first visit to Miki's house.

When Miki appears at the top of the stairs, we stare at

each other for a few tense seconds. She's wearing leggings and an oversized university sweatshirt. Her black hair is in two ponytails.

"Oh, I thought you were Danni-Lynn," she says.

"She said you weren't feeling well."

"Ugh, okay fine, I lied. I didn't want to go to school today, so I told my dad I had cramps. Works every time." Miki sighs as she slowly descends the stairs. When she sees the dog sniffing at my feet, she rushes down to the foyer. "No, Totoro! Bad boy! Stop doing that!"

Totoro lets out a low woof but continues to sniff at my socks. Miki quickly picks him up and puts him under her arm like a loaf of bread.

"Cute dog," I say.

"Thanks." Miki stands in front of me, full of uneasiness. "He's a rescue I saved from death row."

We stare at each other for a few more awkward moments before I speak again.

"I have your homework and your math test."

Miki takes the stack of papers from me. "Aw, Ms. Castillo is letting me flunk this test in the privacy of my home."

"Ocha demo ikaga?"

The elderly man has returned, slowly moving into the family room. He's holding a tray with a bowl of fruit and a porcelain tea set.

"No, Grandpa, she isn't staying for tea," Miki says as he carefully places the tray on the table. "Also this isn't Danni-Lynn. This is Wednesday. She's . . . a new friend."

Miki looks at me as the tips of her ears turn pink. Are we really friends? I've never had any, but I know friends don't keep the truth from each other. The tiny bit of anger plops in my stomach. Miki must sense my feelings because she averts her gaze, looking ashamed.

When Totoro wiggles under her arm and whines, she kisses the top of his head. "Yes, my son, I know it's time."

Miki leaves me in the foyer and quickly returns with a yellow leash clipped to Totoro's harness. When she puts him back on the floor, he wags his tail eagerly.

"I need to take Totoro for his walk," she says. "Do you want to join me?"

"I'm sorry I didn't text or call you," Miki says when we get outside. "I didn't know what to say."

"You could have started with the truth."

She lets out a sad laugh as Totoro takes the lead down Hampshire Avenue. He doesn't waste any time marking his territory.

"I can't believe Alexa came to your house," Miki says.

"She wasn't exactly happy to be there."

Miki looks away from me. "I thought I made the right decision. The club needed a medium, and you lived in the Callahan House. It was a no-brainer. I didn't want to jeopardize that opportunity."

"The right decision?" I stop walking, and Totoro comes to sit by my feet as if he's on my side. "Were you *ever* going to tell me?"

Miki's eyes are full of panic. "I thought—well, you never said anything bad about Violet, so I figured maybe . . . maybe I was right and Alexa was wrong."

"Does Danni-Lynn know what happened?"

Miki shrinks a little at my question. "As president of the club, I took executive privilege to withhold that information from her."

I cross my arms in frustration. "Do you remember how mad Danni-Lynn got when she found out I saw Violet and you didn't tell her about it? She won't be happy when she finds out what happened to Alexa."

"Okay, I know that!" Miki admits. "But Violet would never hurt anyone! She didn't hurt me and Danni-Lynn last Halloween!"

"It's not the same for you!" I tell her. "Wicked ghosts are *very* dangerous to people like Alexa and me."

Miki blinks. "Wicked ghosts?"

Her reaction reminds me she doesn't know what my family calls different types of ghosts. Before Alexa came by my house, I'd planned to share those details at the next club meeting. But I didn't think I would need to tell them about the wicked ones at all. When I explain what they are to Miki and what happened to me in Arizona, her face turns pale.

"You mean they possess you?" she whispers. "Like . . . like a demon?"

"Now do you understand why Alexa didn't want to help Violet? She was afraid!"

Miki bites her lip. "Violet isn't one of those wicked ghost things."

"Wicked ghosts are shape-shifters too," I tell her. "They steal faces from the dead. This one has been using Violet's appearance."

"No, Violet isn't some shape-shifter. She's *real*."

Miki's face is full of denial. She doesn't want to accept Violet is a wicked ghost. I know I won't be able to convince her of the truth. She'll never believe the ghost who spoke to her on Halloween wasn't her best friend. Nothing I can say will change that.

"Violet may have crossed over already." My voice is lower now and less angry. "She may have left the day she—"

"Violet wouldn't leave us without saying goodbye." Miki's voice shakes.

Totoro rises from the sidewalk and tugs at the leash. Miki lets him lead the way to finish his business, and we walk down Sinclair Street and cross over to Hampshire Avenue back toward Miki's house.

"Ghosts don't always say goodbye before they leave," I say, remembering the ghost of Tatiana Hensley, who crossed over without saying goodbye to her older sister, Patricia.

We're now standing in front of Miki's house. She looks tired and sad. She's kept the club going because of Violet. She's done everything she could to help her best friend— even some wrong things. But it's only because she wanted to honor Violet's last request.

"I'm sorry I kept this from you. I'll understand if you don't want to be our medium anymore," Miki says solemnly. "But I didn't lie to you about Violet. She was a good person and would never hurt anyone. When she died, it was the worst thing to ever happen to me."

Miki stops speaking and her eyes fill up with tears. I'm witnessing her grief again. The pain of loss. I don't say anything. I've learned silence is better. Words don't hold the same power as presence.

"I should have told you the truth about Alexa before you took the oath." Miki wipes the tears from her face. "I'll tell Danni-Lynn about Alexa tonight."

The easiest thing to do would be to quit the Dead Club. I've only known Miki and Danni-Lynn for a few weeks. Alexa has made it clear she doesn't want anything to do with me. I'm used to not having friends—even though the thought of eating alone in the cafeteria or hiding away in the library makes my chest ache. But I could do it. I could push everything and everyone away until my gift fades—and then the dead and their unfinished business wouldn't matter at all.

But now I know about Caleb Callahan and the protection he provides inside Nana's house. If the wicked ghost is still in Alton, it can no longer hurt me.

My brain stirs with another possibility, and it snaps into place like a missing puzzle piece. Violet asked the Dead Club to contact the Callahan ghost. Maybe she knew Caleb could banish the wicked ghost. Maybe Miki and Danni-Lynn talked with the *real* Violet after all.

Miki's voice rushes back into my ears. ". . . No matter what your decision is about the club, I hope we can still be friends. I know that's probably not going to happen, but I would like to be your friend."

She waits for my response as if she's ready to accept I'm leaving the Dead Club and ending our friendship.

"Miki, I believe what Alexa told me," I tell her quietly. "But I also believe you too. I've learned something about Caleb Callahan, and it's making me think Violet may have wanted the club to contact him for a specific reason—I can share everything at our next meeting so we can all be on the same page."

Miki's eyes fill up with happy tears. "So . . . you're staying in the club as our medium?"

When I nod, she hurls into me and hugs me tight. "Thank you, Wednesday! I promise never to keep anything from you ever again."

CHAPTER TWENTY

Over the next week, I only make contact with the living.

The mental storms and anxious feelings I experienced when I first came to Alton have disappeared. I'm not afraid of the dead anymore, and I feel safe knowing the Callahan ghost protects Nana's house. But the puzzle still floats around in my brain. Even though I don't think I'm missing any more pieces—there's a nagging tug that tells me I haven't fully solved it.

At the next club meeting, Danni-Lynn takes notes as I share what I've learned about Caleb and my experience with wicked ghosts. Although Miki believes Violet hasn't crossed over, I tell her if the ghost doesn't appear on Halloween, she may have to accept that Violet is in the spirit realm.

The neighborhood has fully embraced the spooky season. The trees have surrendered their colors, and now there's the crunch of leaves under my sneakers. Even though I can wear light jackets and hoodies without sweating, the air in Alton doesn't have the cold bite of Boston or the cool dryness of Las Vegas.

Jasmine and Lincoln carved pumpkins and decorated

the steps, and Olivia used leftover sheet metal to make creepy designs to hang from the porch ceiling—spiders, skulls, and skeletons. We painted them in different hues of black, yellow, and orange. Now Nana's house actually looks haunted.

Since Alexa revealed her experience with the wicked ghost, I no longer keep a vigil at my window for Violet. Instead each night after I finish my homework, I wait for Caleb to make an appearance. Sometimes I talk to Miki or Danni-Lynn on the phone as I keep watch, but then the disappointment presses on my chest when the ghost doesn't show up.

Tonight, I feel that same heaviness as I push my braids into my bonnet and get into bed. I stare at the ceiling as the house settles with its familiar creaks.

My eyes grow heavy with each breath, and soon I let go of the mystery of the Callahan ghost.

It's past midnight when Olivia shakes me awake.

I blink the confused mask of sleep from my eyes, and it takes me a moment to realize it wasn't Olivia who woke me up—I'm alone in the room.

Shivering in bed, I wrap the comforter tight around my body. The room is freezing, and I scan my surroundings. In the corner by the nightstand, a dark shadow moves toward me.

I scramble away to the other side of my bed. Not a shadow, but a person. No, not a person. A ghost.

Caleb Callahan moves to the foot of the bed. He was

thirteen when he died, but in death, he looks much younger and smaller. The street lamppost highlights his face, and a nasty bruise wraps around his neck—the imprint of the wicked ghost forever marked on his skin. The one who used his father's strong hands to take his life.

My throat goes dry, and everything in my body tells me I should scream—but I know who's in my room, so I'm not afraid. Not anymore.

"Caleb?" I whisper.

He cocks his head at the mention of his name. I slowly pull down the comforter from my chin. The air is icy when I take a breath to calm my excitement.

"I'm Wednesday," I tell him. "Olivia's daughter."

When Caleb doesn't react, I frown. Did he forget who she was? I swallow my doubt and try another name.

"Olivia is Lucille's daughter." I pause when he remains unblinking. "Lucille was Josephine's daughter."

The ghost reacts to Nana's name and takes another step toward the bed. I feel like I should pay some kind of respect to this ghost, so I bow my head in reverence to the dead boy.

"Thank you for letting me stay in your house and in your room."

When I look back up at him, he gives me a nod as if he understands what I've said and has accepted my appreciation.

Caleb turns toward the window, and I follow his gaze. The ghost raises his hand and points as if he wants me to go look.

I pull the comforter off me and stand on wobbly legs—the hardwood floor is as cold as a sheet of ice. I slowly venture past Caleb Callahan, the unblinking dead boy in pajamas, until I'm at the window and looking at the house across the street.

In an upstairs room, a lamp shines bright in the darkness.

The Leehans are still away in Spain. No one should be inside their house—especially at this time of night.

The lamp turns off.

I squint my eyes as if I've just seen a mirage, but I know what I've seen is real. After a few racing heartbeats, the lamp turns on again. Three pulses of light repeat several times—some of them faster than others. A pattern I don't understand. The room turns dark again, and the lamp doesn't turn back on.

I can't feel the cold of my room anymore, and I hold my breath, waiting for something to happen.

In the house across the street, the curtains slowly part, and a hand appears in the window—a single palm pressing against the glass. A ghost has made contact with me.

When the hand disappears, my brain fizzes with questions. Could this ghost be Violet? The *real* Violet? Has she been inside her house this entire time?

When I turn around to thank the Callahan ghost for waking me, he's already gone. The hardwood floor is balmy under my bare feet. I search the corners of my room, but Caleb has gone elsewhere.

CHAPTER TWENTY-ONE

It takes everything for me to wait until I can speak to both members of the Dead Club in the cafeteria. But to keep my word to the oath, I'll have to be creative about it.

When I approach the high-top table, Miki and Danni-Lynn are leaning close together and looking at a math worksheet.

"I'll never meet a denominator in real life." Miki rolls her eyes. "And fractions don't seem like nice people."

"That's because fractions are not people." Danni-Lynn lets out a weary sigh. "They're numbers."

"I hate numbers," Miki grumbles. "What makes them so special?"

"How about eighth grade?" Danni-Lynn points at the worksheet. "You know you can't fail this class."

Miki looks at me for support, and I shrug. "She's right. But Danni-Lynn is the perfect person to help you."

Danni-Lynn continues to vouch for the importance of math in the real world, and Miki puts her head down on the table and groans in frustration.

I take this opportunity to grab a napkin and write

Caleb's name in all caps. When I've finished writing, I clear my throat and both girls turn to me. I slowly push the napkin to the center of the table, and their eyes grow wide.

"*When?*" Danni-Lynn whispers.

"Last night," I tell her.

"This is *huge!*" Miki bolts up in her chair. "We need to have an emergency meeting."

"We can't have a meeting today," Danni-Lynn says. "As your math mentor, I need to make sure we have our first tutoring session."

"Are you being serious with me right now?" Miki's voice rises an octave.

Danni-Lynn turns to me. "You didn't text us last night, so I'm assuming whatever happened wasn't earth-shattering, right?"

"It was really late." I say. "But Caleb showed me—"

"Remember the oath!" Miki whisper-shouts. "No club business at school."

"Agreed," Danni-Lynn says firmly.

"I'm making an executive decision," Miki says. "This development is a higher priority than anything else. We need to have a meeting *today*."

"Fine," Danni-Lynn says. "Mama is already planning to pick us up after school, so we'll have to do the meeting at my house."

Miki slaps the table in triumph. "Wednesday, you can meet us after school to go to Danni-Lynn's house."

"Okay, I can hang out until you finish your tutoring

session," I say. "After that, I can tell you what happened with Caleb."

"Oh, we'll do the meeting first," Miki says.

"Fractions first," Danni-Lynn corrects her.

"I'm already flunking math. Trying to understand fractions *after* we have a club meeting won't change that."

Danni-Lynn's house has a grand porch and second-level balcony. Painted sherbet orange with green shutters, it's one of several historic homes on Prince Street. Olivia and I have passed by this house several times on the way to downtown Alton.

"I hope y'all want some refreshments," Danni-Lynn's mother says as she gets out of the car. "I didn't know what to get, so I got some of everything!"

"You always have the *best* snacks!" Miki says.

Danni-Lynn's mother smiles widely at each of us. She's wearing a casual outfit—a pin-striped blouse with blue slacks—but it looks expensive and chic. Her blond hair falls down her back in loose waves, and I can see the resemblance to Danni-Lynn in her kind face.

"Wednesday, I've heard so much about you," she says. "I'm so happy to meet you. Welcome to our home." Her heels click on the brick walkway as she guides us to the front door.

We follow behind her, and I move closer to Danni-Lynn. "I didn't know you lived here."

"You didn't know she lived in a whole mansion?" Miki slides between us.

"It's not a mansion," Danni-Lynn quickly says.

But when we enter the house, I gasp at the marble foyer and curved staircase.

Miki giggles at my reaction. "Welcome to the Taylor-Abbott House. Remind me to show you the fancy sign outside."

"Let's go upstairs," Danni-Lynn says. "The sooner we get Miki to understand fractions, the sooner we can talk about Caleb Callahan."

We climb the curved staircase and go to Danni-Lynn's room. This time, it's me who starts giggling after she opens the door.

It's not the pink walls or the pink bed or even the bonus room with the flat-screen TV and fireplace that overwhelm me. It's the posters and framed photos dedicated to *Loveburned*. There's a bookshelf filled with special-edition books. Over her desk, Danni-Lynn has created a collage of photos from the TV series and its cast, but Leo Stacks has an entire wall dedicated to him. I stare at one of his large posters, and I have to admit looking at the British boy's pretty face makes my cheeks burn.

"Is it too much?" Danni-Lynn asks.

"No, it's—"

"I've told her several times, it's too much," Miki interrupts me. "But Danni-Lynn isn't hurting anyone."

I wander around the room and take it all in. Have I ever been this passionate about anything? Maybe helping ghosts—I know so much about them. Although I don't have a room dedicated to the dead, I understand Danni-Lynn's devotion for *Loveburned*.

"There's nothing wrong with having a passion for what you love," I tell her.

Danni-Lynn blushes as she smiles at me. "I'll tutor Miki in the media room, but you can do your homework at my desk. This first mentor session should take about an hour."

"An *hour*?" Miki gapes at her. "How about thirty minutes?"

The math mentoring session lasts only fifteen minutes before Miki starts begging for snacks, and Danni-Lynn reluctantly goes downstairs and returns with several bags of chips.

"Dibs on barbecue," Miki says, grabbing her choice.

I sit on the thick carpet in the media room, and Danni-Lynn opens a cabinet that turns out to be a refrigerator and gives us each a bottle of water.

"Since you don't want to learn today, do you want to call the meeting to order?" she asks Miki.

She nods as she finishes her bag of chips. "Let's talk club business. *Finally*."

We all settle in a tight circle. Danni-Lynn opens the club notebook, and I nervously take a sip of water as Miki brings the meeting to order.

"The Callahan ghost contacted you," Danni-Lynn says. "What did he say?"

"He didn't speak at all."

Danni-Lynn scribbles my response in the club notebook, and Miki eagerly nods for me to continue.

I tell them how Caleb led me to the window, where I saw the blinking lights and the ghostly hand.

"I'm not sure if it was Violet. Her house is almost as old as Nana's, so it could be someone else who died there."

"Wait . . . *wait*." Miki scrambles up from the carpet and starts pacing. "Okay, Wednesday, you said the lamp blinked three times, stopped, and then started over again, right?"

"It was more like a pattern. Sometimes the blinks were really fast. Other times they were slow."

"That's Morse code." Miki pulls out her phone from the back pocket of her jeans. "When Violet and I were little, we used to play around with our flashlights. Her father taught us Morse code, so we could communicate in the dark. It was a game we played in the summertime."

"You think it was Violet who sent Wednesday that message?" Danni-Lynn asks.

Miki nods as her fingers swipe on her phone screen. "I don't know all the codes but . . . here it is. We never used this one." She pauses and looks at both of us. "Three fast blinks followed by three slower ones, then three fast ones again, means SOS. A call for help."

"Does that mean she's in trouble?" Danni-Lynn's voice is full of concern. "Do you think Violet is trapped in her house?"

"She could be a bound ghost. They can't leave the location of their death . . ." I pause as a revelation spreads in my chest. "Except on Halloween."

"We have to do something. Violet is asking for help, and we need to take action," Miki says. "Now that we know where she is, we need to go to her."

"How are we going to do that?" Danni-Lynn asks. "The Leehans live in Violet's house now. They're not going to just let us in—especially if we tell them we need to talk to a ghost."

I think of the hand pressed against the window—almost like a desperate plea. I bite my lip as an idea spins in my brain.

"The Leehans aren't in the house right now," I say.

Miki tilts her head. "The house is empty?"

"They're on vacation in Spain, but they're coming back to Alton on Friday afternoon."

Danni-Lynn's frown turns into a full grimace of disapproval. "You're not talking about breaking and entering, are you? That's a crime."

"My godmother is taking care of their house while they're away, so she has the keys."

Miki grins as she kneels in front of me. "Do you think you could get the keys?"

"We're turning into juvenile delinquents," Danni-Lynn mumbles under her breath as she writes in the club notebook.

"Jasmine usually comes to our house to work on professor stuff," I tell them. "She knows all about my family. If I tell her I need to contact a ghost in the house, maybe she'll understand and give me the keys."

"This is the kind of action I'm talking about." Miki rubs her hands in excitement. "But we only have a day left before the Leehans come back. We have to get those keys tomorrow. As president of the club, I say we move forward on this. Let's take a vote."

When both Miki and I raise our hands, Danni-Lynn shakes her head and closes the club notebook.

"Fine. We can go, but I'm not putting this in the meeting minutes. Keys or not, it's still trespassing."

CHAPTER TWENTY-TWO

The next day after school, I go straight to Nana's house. I let out a sigh of relief when I find Jasmine in the library. She's bobbing her head to music on her headphones. I wave my hands until I get her attention, and she looks up at me with a lopsided grin.

"Had a good day, Wednesday?" she says too loud.

I nod, and Jasmine focuses back on her laptop, clacking on the keyboard and swinging her shoulders to music I can't hear. The Dead Club plans to meet in Violet's backyard in half an hour. More than enough time to ask Jasmine for the keys.

Sensing my stare, Jasmine looks up at me and her hazel eyes scan me for signs of trouble. When she squints with suspicion, she takes off her headphones.

"Everything all right?" she asks.

"If I asked you to do something for me—you would help me out, right?"

Jasmine smirks at me as if we're sharing some kind of secret. "Depends on what you want to do. Is it illegal?"

My face burns. "Of course not."

Jasmine tilts her head. "So why are you being so

secretive? Just ask me. What do you want me to do for you?"

This is harder than I thought it would be. Jasmine knows about ghosts, so I can tell her the truth. But if she tells me no—if she doesn't give me the keys, then I'll have to find another way to get into the Leehans' house. And that *would* be illegal.

"Liv told me about your little Dead Club, by the way." Jasmine closes her laptop. "She also told me about the ghost across the street. Does your favor have to do with any of that?"

"It does." I straighten my posture, standing taller. "I'm the club's medium, and I've been trying to contact Violet—she's the ghost across the street. I need to talk to her."

"Ah, I get it now," Jasmine says. "You need to get inside the Leehans' house."

"Technically it's Violet's house," I correct her and then squirm when she frowns at me. "You know, like Caleb Callahan thinks this house is his?"

"I've been taking care of *two* haunted houses." Jasmine leans back in the leather chair and chuckles. "Woo, I need my own TV show."

"I really need to talk to Violet." I glance at my watch. "In the next twenty minutes."

"Ghosts have a schedule now?"

"She may be in trouble," I plead. "You know I wouldn't ask if this wasn't important."

She gives me a long stare and then nods her head. "Okay, Wednesday."

"Thank you so much! I'll bring the keys right back to—"

"Not so fast, Miss Medium." Jasmine holds up her hand to stop me from talking. "Listen, I promised Marcelle and Nancy nothing bad would happen while they're gone. I'm not letting you go into that house alone."

"But you can trust—"

"It's not that I don't trust you," Jasmine interrupts me again. "You might be able to talk to ghosts, but you're still a kid, Wednesday. You're not going inside that house without me. That's the deal. Take it or leave it."

I open my mouth to protest, but I know it won't be any use. I should be grateful Jasmine is letting me talk to Violet in the first place.

"Okay, but we have to go in the next fifteen minutes," I tell her.

"Wow." Jasmine chuckles again. "Let me finish this last thing, and we can go. You think that will work for your little ghost?"

"I'll meet you outside."

Jasmine rolls her eyes as she shoos me away. I leave the library and pause at the staircase, but then decide I don't need to go upstairs and change clothes. My jeans and T-shirt should be fine—although I do pull off the gray cardigan I'm wearing. The stress of asking Jasmine to help the club has made me too warm.

When I go out on the porch, I look up and down the street. I don't see Danni-Lynn or Miki, but maybe they've already made their way to Violet's backyard.

I pull out my phone and send a text to the Dead Club group chat.

> Wednesday: are you two already over there
> Miki: YES WHERE ARE YOU
> Danni-Lynn: We're 13 minutes early
> Wednesday: on the way
> MIKI: HURRY UP
> Wednesday: change in plans jasmine is coming too
> Miki: WHAT??!! SHE'S NOT A CLUB MEMBER :(
> Danni-Lynn: Did you get us in trouble
> Miki: JASMINE HASN'T TAKEN THE OATH
> Danni-Lynn: Stop shouting Miki
> Wednesday: it's the only way we can get inside the house
> Miki: I DON'T LIKE IT
> Wednesday: sorry
> Danni-Lynn: It's okay
> Miki: I guess this will work
> Danni-Lynn: I'm glad you stopped shouting at us
> Miki: HURRY UP
> Wednesday: see you soon

Jasmine follows me across the street, and I quickly go in the backyard to fetch the girls. On the porch, they huddle close to each other as Jasmine looks them over.

Danni-Lynn has on the same dress she wore to school, but Miki has changed into black track shorts and a red university T-shirt. As Jasmine continues to study them, Danni-Lynn clutches the club notebook to her chest like a shield.

"Didn't realize you invited your club buddies to this séance," Jasmine says as she continues to examine the girls. "You conveniently left that part out."

"They're Violet's friends," I tell her.

Jasmine's face softens in sympathy before she opens the front door. "Let's not tell Liv about this, okay?"

"We're *really* good at keeping secrets," Miki offers.

"Oh, I believe you," Jasmine says as we follow her inside.

The house is cool and quiet. Streaks of sunshine bounce against the wood beams on the ceiling. The air is stale with the faint scent of oregano.

Miki surveys the great room. "Everything looks so different now," she whispers.

Danni-Lynn walks around and stares at the Leehans' furniture and the artwork on the walls. "They have good taste."

"Don't touch anything," Jasmine tells us.

On the fireplace mantel are photos of the couple on their travels. Jasmine points to a few frames, giving us details. The Leehans smiling on a boat in Greece. The women sitting on camels in Egypt. Another photo has the pair hiking through the rainforests of Costa Rica. Other souvenirs clutter around the frames.

There's nothing left of Violet's family here. None of their photos. No mementos. Only the bones of house. I wonder if the ghost has been lonely.

"We should go to Violet's room," Miki says. "That would be the best place to start."

We climb the split-level stairs, and Miki moves forward and points to the first room on the left. Jasmine opens the door to reveal yellow walls with white trim. There's a small iron bed with a butterfly comforter, along with a small dresser and a nightstand covered with candles.

"Violet liked butterflies," Danni-Lynn whispers.

Miki scratches her arm. "It's too bare, and she doesn't have anything in here to read."

I move to the window and stare at Nana's house and then up at my room. How many nights had Violet stood here in the darkness and watched me? Turning back to the nightstand, I turn on the lamp—the same one the ghost used to signal the SOS message.

The girls sit on the floor next to the bed. They both watch me, waiting for instructions.

"So, how does this work?" Jasmine leans against the doorway. "Should we light a candle to let the ghost know we're here?"

"No," I say quietly. "Violet knows we're here. Now we wait."

Danni-Lynn opens the club notebook and scans the room nervously. Miki twists the bottom of her T-shirt with her hands. Jasmine continues to stare at the candles on the nightstand. None of them will see Violet if she appears.

I sit on the bed and close my eyes. Violet beckoned me to her house. If she knows I'm here waiting, she'll make her presence known. At least that's my hope.

When the temperature drops in the room, I open my eyes. A figure looms in the doorway behind Jasmine, and I rise from the bed.

No sparks ignite in my brain. No gathering clouds or churning storms. Spikes of fear don't leap in my chest. I don't feel any danger. Only a deep certainty that a ghost needs our help.

CHAPTER TWENTY-THREE

Violet looks like the ghost I've seen before—wearing the same overall shorts and T-shirt.

"That girl is here, isn't she?" Jasmine asks.

She can't see Violet, but it doesn't stop her from shivering in the doorway as the ghost passes by her.

Miki and Danni-Lynn's eyes are wide with anticipation, but they also can't see their best friend. The only sign of Violet's presence is the frigid air swirling in the room.

I turn to Jasmine. "Can you give us some privacy?"

She frowns. "You're kidding, right?"

"They haven't talked to Violet in a long time," I quickly tell her. "I don't want them to feel embarrassed about it."

Jasmine looks at Miki and Danni-Lynn sitting on the floor, and her face softens again in sympathy. "Okay, but I'm gonna be *right* outside."

When the door closes, Violet moves closer to the bed and stares at her friends sitting on the floor. A mix of joy and sadness appears on her face.

"I can tell them anything you want them to know," I say gently.

"Violet?" Miki leans forward, her eyes filling with tears. "Where are you?"

"She's right in front of you," I answer.

The ghost looks at me and now the only emotion I see is sorrow. "Can you tell them I miss them?"

I turn to Danni-Lynn and Miki. "Violet says she misses you."

Miki's face turns stricken and the tears she's been holding fall down her face. Danni-Lynn sniffs and pulls out a tissue to give to Miki.

After Violet sees their reactions, she looks at me. "Thanks for bringing them with you."

"You've been in this house the whole time, haven't you?" I ask.

"Yes." Violet's voice is low and angry. "This is the first time we've met."

I pull my arms close to my chest, and a sense of dread settles on my shoulders.

Miki leans forward. "What did she say?"

"This is the real Violet," I tell her. "I've never spoken to her before now."

Danni-Lynn opens the club notebook, and her pen hovers over a blank page. "Wednesday, I'm going to try to write down everything y'all say to each other."

I nod and take a deep breath. "Violet, my name is Wednesday Thomas. I'm Josephine Marlow's great-granddaughter. When I moved here last month, I met a ghost with your face, and I offered to find out what happened to your parents. I thought I was trying to help you."

"It was the bad thing." Violet narrows her eyes. "It got inside me and it felt like it was pressing me down. When I pushed it out, I felt . . . different, like it had taken something from me."

My memory takes me back to the Arizona state park. I'm on the warm, wet ground. Dark slivers enter my body, and a heavy weight presses on my chest.

I shudder as the dark forest disappears. I'm back in the yellow bedroom, and Violet stares at me.

"It stole my face, my clothes . . . everything about me," she says. "I think that's what it wanted."

"The bad thing that possessed you—my family calls it a wicked ghost," I tell her.

Since wicked ghosts are so deformed and decayed, they have to steal from the dead to trick the living who can see them. The wicked ghost in Arizona used the disguise of a lost child to lure me into the dark forest.

Danni-Lynn tugs the leg of my jeans. "Wednesday, let us know what Violet is telling you."

When I share what I've learned, Danni-Lynn exchanges a shocked look with Miki before she scribbles furiously in the club notebook. Violet sits next to me on the bed, slumping her shoulders.

"When I first woke up, I was so confused because I was alone. I tried to leave, but every time I opened the door, I would just end up back in the house. That's when

I realized . . . I was dead. Then one night, I was able to go outside."

I give Violet a sad smile. The opportunity for her to wander in the world of the living only happened on one sacred night.

"You're bound to this house. Ghosts like you can only leave the place they died on Halloween," I say.

"That's when the bad thing got me. After I pushed it out, I knew something bad had happened, but I didn't know what to do." Violet's voice is bitter with disappointment. "Caleb Callahan was the most dangerous ghost I knew, and I thought he could help me hunt the bad thing down. But I couldn't find him, and I didn't think I could go inside his house, so I just sat on my porch. That's when I saw Miki and Danni-Lynn, and I knew they could get Alexa to contact him. But I left them because I wanted to see if I could find the bad thing myself . . . I never did. Then I was back here again."

My chest aches listening to her story, but I know she deserves to hear the truth about Alexa. "There's something you need to know, Violet."

After I tell her what happened to Alexa, Violet doesn't speak for a moment.

"Does she hate me now?" she asks. "Is that why she isn't here?"

"She doesn't hate you," I say.

Her eyes fill with desperate hope. "Can you help me? I . . . I don't want anything bad to happen to anyone else."

"Halloween is only a few nights away," I tell her. "That's why your form has gotten stronger, and why you could contact me with the lamp."

"Will I be able to go outside again?"

I nod and then tell her about Caleb Callahan and how she was right to ask the Dead Club to contact him. "He can banish the wicked ghost."

Relief floods Violet's face. "Thank you, Wednesday."

Miki rises from her spot on the floor. "On Halloween, we'll meet you outside. We'll use the same SOS signal so you'll know it's us."

Danni-Lynn is scribbling the last of our exchange when Jasmine gives a quick knock and opens the door.

"Okay, y'all. Séance time is over," she says, shivering from the cold.

Violet rises from the bed, giving each of us one last look before she passes Jasmine and disappears into the hallway.

None of us says anything as we follow Jasmine down the stairs. Danni-Lynn clutches the club notebook to her chest—now filled with the recorded words of her dead best friend.

Outside on the porch, Jasmine locks the door. "The Leehans will be back in town tomorrow, so don't get any fancy ideas that we'll be doing this again anytime soon."

We walk across the street, but we linger at the gate, letting Jasmine go up the porch steps alone. It's not until she enters Nana's house that anyone dares to speak.

"I took a *lot* of notes," Danni-Lynn says. "But I feel like we're missing something. . . ."

Miki leans forward. "What are you thinking?"

"If that bad ghost attacked Alexa, then why hasn't it tried the same thing with Wednesday? It knows she's a medium too."

"Maybe it knows about Caleb," Miki says. "Maybe that's why it's staying away from Wednesday."

"Caleb is a bound ghost like Violet," I say. "I'm not sure the wicked ghost even knows about him unless it entered the house, and it definitely hasn't done that yet."

"Maybe it's found someone else it likes better," Danni-Lynn says.

A cold dread washes over me when I think about an innocent person being devoured by the wicked ghost. Their body stolen from them and no longer theirs. A hostage of their own life—family and friends unaware of the impostor moving among them.

"We can talk about banishing this ghost later," Miki says. "We need to talk to Alexa. She needs to know the truth about Violet."

CHAPTER TWENTY-FOUR

The next day at school, we wait in the courtyard for Alexa. Our stakeout is the stone round table closest to the main entrance. Miki nervously taps her leg as she scans groups of girls entering Noble Middle School. Danni-Lynn works on math homework, her pencil making confident strokes as she solves equations. I sit between them, my hands folded in my lap. Every few moments, I take a deep breath, but it doesn't make me feel calm—I'm full of fizzy stress. What will Alexa do? Will she return to the club? Will she help us banish the wicked ghost?

Miki's leg continues to bounce against me. "Maybe we've already missed her. Should we check her homeroom?"

"We got here really early," I say. "She's not here yet."

"What if she's out sick today?"

Danni-Lynn huffs. "Alexa doesn't play sick like you do."

Miki turns to her. "Hey, no jokes from you. Finish my homework, please."

"Just know I'm solving some of these fractions wrong, and it hurts my whole heart," Danni-Lynn says, pouting. "But we don't need Ms. Castillo thinking you've turned into a math genius yet. Way too suspicious."

I spot Alexa in the courtyard with a group of eighth-grade girls and other spirit squad members. They're wearing their blue-and-gold outfits. Alexa's hair is in two coily buns—the same hairstyle she had on my first day of school. When I touch Miki's leg, she straightens up at the table.

"Hey y'all!" Danni-Lynn waves.

While the other girls smile and wave back, Alexa frowns and walks faster, moving ahead of them. She quickly disappears through the school's entrance.

"She doesn't want to talk to us," I say.

Miki rises from the table and marches after Alexa. Danni-Lynn and I exchange worried glances, and we quickly scoop up our things. My stomach flutters with nerves when we go through the school doors, but Miki and Alexa are nowhere to be seen. Our classmates move around us, and Danni-Lynn bites her lip in worry.

"Where did they go?" she asks me.

I walk past the wall of trophy cases to the main hallway. The wavering form of Terrance Sims glimmers under the fluorescent lights.

When the wisp ghost's memory loop ends, I know where Miki and Alexa have gone, and I take Danni-Lynn's hand.

I guide her to the hallway bathroom. When I push open the door, Miki and Alexa are arguing in front of the sinks.

"Why are you always like this?" Miki says. "Stop being so stubborn and listen to what I have to say to you!"

"You have some nerve!" Alexa snaps. "You're the queen

of Stubborn Kingdom! You won't leave me alone when I've made it clear I want *nothing* to do with you or *your* club."

"Good lord, Alexa," Danni-Lynn says. "Can you just listen to what Miki has to say?"

When Alexa sees me, she lets out an irritated laugh. "I can't believe you're still with them—after *everything* I told you. Miki doesn't care about you; she doesn't understand what it's like for us!"

The bathroom door opens again, and a sixth grader in a polka-dot jumpsuit looks at all of us before Danni-Lynn gently shoos the confused girl out.

"So sorry, honey," Danni-Lynn drawls. "We're having an important secret meeting right now. Go pee in the bathroom in the next hallway."

The sixth grader widens her eyes and darts out. Danni-Lynn turns back to us, leaning against the bathroom door. "No one else comes in here until we finish this conversation."

"I thought we—what happened to *no club business at school*?" Alexa's voice cracks in disbelief. "What happened to the second part of the oath?!"

"As president of the club, I've just declared an executive order. For special circumstances, club business can be discussed at school," Miki says.

"Of course you would do that." Alexa narrows her eyes. "You always do what *you* want."

Miki's face draws up in surprise. "What do you mean by that? Everything I've ever done has been for the club and for Violet! Too bad I can't say the same thing for you. You stopped hanging out with us. Stopped talking to us. You abandoned us after Violet died! You—you were being selfish!"

Alexa lets out another irritated laugh, but this one has a hint of darkness to it. "Oh, I was being selfish?"

My stomach clenches in knots as I move forward to get between them—to stop them from shouting at each other—but Danni-Lynn pulls me back.

"This has been a long time coming," she tells me. "They need to have this reckoning with each other. Let them work it out."

"You were the one being selfish," Alexa continues. "You took all of Violet's stuff from her room. You didn't ask me or Danni-Lynn if we wanted anything. Instead you made yourself club president and made that scary shrine at your house. You didn't even ask us how we felt about it."

"I took Violet's things from her room to *save* them," Miki protests. "Her parents were going to give it all away! You could have had anything you wanted, but you stopped coming to the meetings!"

Alexa crosses her arms. "Why can't you just leave me alone, Miki?"

"Because I need to talk to you about Violet!"

"I already told you Violet is dangerous." Alexa's voice is tight with anger. "You know what she is, but all you care about is the club! You never asked me once if I was okay!"

"How can I ask if you're okay when you won't talk to

me!" Miki voice cracks before she bursts into tears.

This time when I move forward, Danni-Lynn doesn't stop me. Miki slowly wipes her tears from her blotchy face as I stand between the girls.

"Alexa, we talked to Violet yesterday," I say quietly. "The *real* Violet."

She blinks. "What?"

"It's true," Danni-Lynn says from the door. "We went to her house."

When I tell Alexa what happened to Violet, she doesn't say anything. Instead, her face crumples into confusion and she moves away from me until she hits the bathroom wall.

No one says anything for a few moments, and when Alexa looks up at us, the anger has disappeared from her eyes.

Miki joins Alexa on the wall. When she leans her head on Alexa's shoulder, Alexa doesn't move away.

"I'm sorry I didn't believe you," Miki whispers.

"I'm sorry too," Alexa says. "I should have answered your texts."

Danni-Lynn stops guarding the door and leans against the wall on the other side of Alexa. I don't move from my spot near the sink. I feel too much like an outsider to join them—even if I've been the one to bring them back together.

"Now that you know the truth about Violet, you can come back to the club," Miki says. "Two mediums will be better than one."

Alexa visibly stiffens before moving away from Miki. "Thanks for telling me about Violet, but I'm not coming back to the club."

When she meets my eyes, I see a painful loss, and a familiar emotion flares up in my chest—a tiny but growing panic.

Miki grabs Alexa's arm. "I don't understand—"

"Maybe she needs to think about it some more," Danni-Lynn suggests. "Let's give her some time."

"Okay, that seems fair," Miki quickly agrees. "The club is here for you, Alexa."

After Alexa leaves the bathroom, Danni-Lynn gives Miki a tight hug and smooths down her hair. Miki washes her face and gets her math homework. We walk into the hallway as if nothing dramatic has happened, and the girls go their separate ways to their homerooms.

I stay behind and wait for the wisp ghost's cold calm to wash over me. The small panic expands in my chest—the fear of losing my gift.

But what I saw in Alexa's eyes wasn't fear. It was the sadness of what she's already lost.

Alexa can no longer see the dead.

CHAPTER TWENTY-FIVE

After school, I walk through the courtyard toward the park. When a voice calls my name, I'm surprised to see Alexa trotting across the grass. She's changed from her spirit squad uniform into her volleyball practice clothes.

"Are you on your way home?" she asks.

When I nod, Alexa fidgets with her gym bag and scans the courtyard. No one is paying us any attention.

"You mind if I walk with you?"

"Oh." I try to hide the surprise. "You won't be late for practice?"

"We're just doing drills, it'll be okay."

My brain fills with many things I want to say, but it isn't until we cross over to Noble Avenue that I feel brave enough to speak.

"I'm glad you and Miki made up," I say.

"We're both stubborn," Alexa tells me. "We should have done that a long time ago."

The wind whooshes a swirl of leaves across our path. I tuck my braids into my jacket before I take the plunge with what I say next.

"It's going to happen to me too."

Alexa keeps walking and doesn't look at me, but I know she's listening.

"It starts slowly at first," I continue, repeating Olivia's words. "Then it stops, and you can't see ghosts anymore. My mother lost her gift after she got her period. I got mine this summer, so it's just a matter of time for me."

As we approach Nana's house, I spot a parked car with an open trunk. Several pieces of luggage lie scattered on the sidewalk. The Leehans have returned from Spain.

We stop at the gate. A few days ago, Olivia decorated it with spiderwebs she made from yarn and cotton for Halloween.

"It happened last November for me," Alexa whispers. "I thought I would be relieved after everything that happened with Violet, but I got really sad. Do you think that's weird?"

"No, it's not weird. I'll be sad when it happens to me too," I say.

I stare at the house across the street and look up at the bedroom window. I wonder if Violet is watching us now. I wait for the ghost to give me a sign, but the curtains don't move.

When the Leehans come out on the porch, the sound of their happy conversation travels across the street. The women wave at us, and Alexa slumps in disappointment as she watches them take their luggage inside the house. Now I realize why she asked if she could walk home with me.

"We can't talk to Violet now that they're back from their trip," I tell her. "I'm sorry."

"I can't believe she's been in her house this whole time," she says softly.

This isn't the same Alexa I know from school. She's not hiding how she feels or dodging questions. I move closer and decide to take advantage of this moment.

"How did Violet find out you could see ghosts?"

Alexa leans against the gate and smiles at the memory. "We were in fourth grade, and I was talking to this *annoying* kid on the playground. He was a ghost, of course. I was mad at him because he wouldn't leave me alone. Violet must have been watching me. When she asked me about it later, I just told her the truth. She didn't even bat an eye. Next thing I know, I get an invitation to her club."

We stand at the gate for a few more moments. Olivia has always told me other people like us exist, but I've never met any. Sometimes I wonder if my life would be different if we never moved to Boston and stayed in Alton. How different would things be for me? I would have grown up across the street from Violet. She would have invited me to the Dead Club. Maybe Alexa and I would have been friends.

I'm not sure if that life would have been better, but at least I could try to be friends with Alexa now.

"Hey, do you want to come up to my room?"

When we enter the house, Olivia's bad singing meets us at the door.

"You remember my mother, right?"

Alexa gives me a small grin. "Does your mom know she can't sing?"

"Oh, she knows." I laugh. "But it doesn't stop her from terrorizing my ears."

"I heard that, Wednesday!"

Olivia arrives from the den wearing one of her paint-splattered jumpers. When she notices Alexa, she raises her eyebrows and smiles.

"It's so good to see you again, Alexa," Olivia says. "My offer is still open for dinner. I can make one of my famous casseroles."

Alexa fidgets next to me, and I wonder if she's thinking about the last time she was here and tried to warn me about Violet.

"She just came over for a short visit." I take Alexa's hand and guide her to the staircase. "We'll be upstairs."

Olivia gives me a thumbs-up before going back into the den.

In my room, I let Alexa sit at my desk while I perch on the bed. I haven't decorated my room yet, and now my face burns in embarrassment as she surveys the bare walls. Alexa probably thinks my room is boring.

"I'm not used to all this space, so everything is still a work in progress," I say.

"I heard you lived in an RV."

"Does everyone at school know my entire story?"

"I also heard you were homeless, but I squashed that

rumor. You're welcome." Alexa lets out an amused huff. "Anyway, you're lucky. I have to share a room with my little sister, and she's kind of a brat."

"How old is your sister?" I ask.

"Darla is eight going on eighty," she laughs.

"Has she seen any ghosts yet?"

The smile disappears from Alexa's face, and I'm afraid I've overstepped a boundary. But she doesn't seem mad at me for asking about her sister.

"I'm adopted, so . . . she isn't like me," Alexa says. "Also . . . my family doesn't know about the ghost thing."

I stare at her with a new respect. Alexa had to figure out everything about the dead by herself while also keeping it a secret from her family.

"You weren't scared when you saw your first one?" I whisper.

Alexa leans back in the chair. "I've seen ghosts all my life, so I didn't know I should be afraid. I thought everyone could see them, but I learned fast that wasn't true. I was more scared of people finding out about me than about the ghosts."

"Do Miki and Danni-Lynn know you're adopted?" I carefully ask.

"I told the club when I found out about it. My parents shared my birth mother's information with me, but I don't know if I got the ghost thing from her. It's not like they would put that kind of stuff in the paperwork."

"Your birth father could have given it to you," I say.

"I guess it doesn't matter now." Alexa's eyes fill with the same sadness from this morning. "I wish I had met someone like you when I was younger. It would have made things much easier."

I want to tell Alexa everything about Lodestars and all the ghosts I've helped. I want to tell her about Nana's rare lifetime gift, but there's too much sorrow on Alexa's face. I don't want to share things that will trigger reminders of what she's lost.

"When I was younger, I wished I had friends who knew what I could do," I say instead. "Maybe I wouldn't have been so lonely."

"I guess we both missed out on some things," Alexa whispers.

We sit in silence in my empty room, but it doesn't feel awkward—there's no pressure for us to fill the quiet with conversation. I'm glad Alexa has opened up to me about her life. The familiar warmth rises in me again—the same emotion I've felt with Miki and Danni-Lynn.

"When do you think you'll be able to talk to Violet again?" Alexa asks.

"Right now, she's bound to her house, but on Halloween she can leave, and as a believer, you'll be able to talk to her yourself."

Alexa's forehead creases in worry. "Why did that wicked ghost steal Violet's face?"

"These types of ghosts have to hide who they are—that's how they can trick you," I tell her. "But they have to change into their true form before they can possess you."

Alexa squirms a little, as if she's trying to push away something unpleasant.

"That's . . . what happened to me. I really thought I was talking to Violet. I was so happy to finally see her. Then she started to change. I've never been so afraid in my entire life."

I see the pure terror in her eyes, and I reach out and squeeze her hand.

"Alexa, how were you able to fight off the wicked ghost?" I gently ask. "Did you follow a light to safety? My family calls it a Lodestar—it takes our souls to a place of protection. Is . . . is that what you used to get away?"

Alexa slowly shakes her head. "No, I . . . I didn't see any bright light. It was pitch-black and I couldn't see anything. It was terrifying, Wednesday."

My throat goes dry. Alexa didn't have a Lodestar to protect her soul from the wicked ghost. It left on its own. I fight a small shudder as I think about what would have happened if it had chosen to stay. For whatever reason, the wicked ghost decided not to steal her life and moved on.

"I'm sorry that happened to you," I whisper. "I'm glad you're safe now."

Alexa gives me a small smile, but I can tell talking about the experience has rattled her. I feel a twinge of regret asking about her possession. Now I realize having a Lodestar may be a rare power among those who can see the dead.

"Are you still planning to help Violet banish the wicked ghost?" Alexa asks.

"The club is going to talk about it on Monday," I tell her. "You should come to the meeting."

Alexa stiffens and pulls her hand away from me. "Sorry, I can't."

When she rises from my desk, I try to hide my disappointment. Alexa still doesn't want to be a part of the club. I want to tell her it doesn't matter that she can't see ghosts anymore. But most of all, I want us to be friends.

Alexa picks up her gym bag and her eyes fill up with a mixture of sadness and concern. "I should go before I miss practice."

I don't try to convince Alexa to come to the club meeting. Instead I give her a long hug and lead her out of my room and down to the front door.

"You can come and visit me again," I tell her. "I would like that."

"Please be careful, Wednesday," Alexa says before she leaves.

PART THREE
A WICKED GHOST

CHAPTER TWENTY-SIX

When I arrive at the clubhouse, I see only Miki's shoes outside. After I place my sneakers beside them, I knock at the door.

Miki doesn't greet me with a hello but with an explanation. "Danni-Lynn is going to be late. She had to do something with one of her school clubs. You would think *this* club would be more important."

Miki's hair is out of its French braid, but she's still wearing her cuffed jeans and the orange-blossom blouse I like. She's already set a pitcher of red punch and a tray of cookies on the table.

I sink into the beanbag chair and inspect the small, cozy place with a new perspective. When I was invited to the club's meet and greet, I thought everything here belonged to Miki, but now I know most of these possessions belonged to Violet.

Miki picks up the tray from the table and offers it to me. "Want one?"

When I bite into the double–chocolate chip cookie, I perk up with surprise. "This is good, Miki."

She beams in pride. "That means a lot coming from you, since I'm sure Beloved Bakery cookies *live* at your house."

"We do have a lot of those turquoise boxes lying around," I admit.

I wonder if I should tell Miki that Alexa can't see ghosts anymore. But it's not my place, so I decide not to reveal it. Alexa will have to tell Miki herself.

"Can I ask you a question?" I ask instead. "Why did Violet choose that book for the oath?"

Miki goes to a bookshelf and pulls out *Wait Till Helen Comes*. She holds it to her chest like a prize, but then she frowns at me. "Ugh, Wednesday. Did you even read it?"

"I've been busy," I say.

"You *have* been busy with ghosts."

Miki flops on the sofa and flips through the pages, and I wait for her to gather her thoughts. "Molly—that's the main character's name, since you didn't read it. . . ."

"Stop giving me a hard time and tell me why Violet loved this book so much."

Miki moves to the edge of the sofa and grins at me. "First off, no one believed Molly when she told them about Helen's ghost. Her mom didn't believe her. Her brother didn't believe her either. Did that stop Molly? Nope. Not even when things got scary. She became her own hero. I think that's why Violet wanted us to take the club oath on it. She knew it didn't matter if no one believed us. We believed in ourselves."

We both turn to a faint knock at the door. Miki gets up from the sofa and lets Danni-Lynn into the clubhouse. She's still wearing her corduroy dress and tights from school.

After grabbing a cookie from the tray, she bounces happily on the sofa. "Did y'all miss me? Tell the truth."

"Of course we missed you. How are the math nerds?" Miki asks.

"They're fine," Danni-Lynn drawls. "They're not failing tests and they're doing their own homework."

"Hey, I got a seventy-four on my last math test!" Miki protests. "Ms. Castillo even put a smiley face on my paper."

The girls continue to tease each other as they settle on the couch. After Danni-Lynn eats two cookies, she opens the club notebook.

"Let's call this meeting to order," Miki announces.

Danni-Lynn flips through several pages of notes. "Okay, according to today's agenda, we need to discuss how we plan to hunt a wicked ghost and get it inside the Callahan House so we can banish it. Goodness, that sounds really bad when you say it out loud."

"Don't forget about Violet," Miki says. "She'll be with us on Halloween, so she can help us track it down."

"Wednesday, has Caleb contacted you again?" Danni-Lynn asks.

"No, he hasn't, but if we bring the wicked ghost inside the house, he'll take care of it."

Danni-Lynn writes my response in the club notebook before she looks up at me. "Maybe the wicked thing is gone, and we don't need to worry about it anymore."

"I believe it's still here," I say.

The girls wait for me to explain. Since we talked to

Violet, a new puzzle has formed in my brain, but this time I think I have all the pieces.

"When I first met Laura Tarkington, she wanted me to help her find out the reason the other school ghosts were hiding. I didn't want to admit it at the time, but the wicked ghost was the reason. The last time I saw her in the cafeteria, she looked really scared, and now I think she's gone into hiding too. They all sense a threat. This is why I think the wicked ghost hasn't found another host yet."

"Do you think the other ghosts will come out on Halloween?" Miki asks.

"I don't know," I admit. "But if they do, then Laura Tarkington will come out of hiding too. As a guide ghost, she might have information for us."

As Danni-Lynn records our conversation in the club notebook, I take a deep breath and gather up the courage to share my plan.

"Since we need to get the wicked ghost inside the house with Caleb, maybe I can lure it there."

Danni-Lynn stops writing. "No, Wednesday. Absolutely not. What if it *possesses* you?"

"I can use my Lodestar," I tell her.

I don't share with them that my Lodestar takes me to a safe place only if I follow its guiding light. I wasn't sure what would happen if I didn't follow its protection route right away.

Danni-Lynn shakes her head. "It's too much of a risk. What if that thing possesses you and then runs away in your body?"

"That's not how wicked ghosts work. It won't run away—it'll want to take over my life and pretend to be me," I tell her. "Listen, Caleb is the reason I came back to Alton. If I can get the wicked ghost inside the house, I trust Caleb can banish it."

Danni-Lynn bites her lip, and Miki furrows her brow in concern. Neither girl likes my plan.

"This may be the only way," I tell them. "A wicked ghost stays on this plane because it wants to live in a physical body. If it hasn't found a host it likes yet, maybe it could still be interested in me."

"I don't like this idea either, Wednesday," Miki says. "Maybe we can figure out another way to get the wicked ghost inside the Callahan House without you getting possessed."

"Halloween is in *three days*," Danni-Lynn says.

"Maybe Violet or the other school ghosts can give us some other ideas," Miki tells her. "For now, let's vote on it."

As long as there's a possibility the wicked ghost isn't gone, both the living and the dead won't be safe. What if there's someone like Alexa who doesn't have a Lodestar to protect them from danger? What about the other ghosts who are hiding? The wicked ghost would be a threat to everyone if it continued to roam free.

"I'm in," I say.

Danni-Lynn looks at both of us and lets out a long groan. "Fine, but I'm going to make it very clear in the meeting minutes that I *strongly* disapprove of this plan."

CHAPTER TWENTY-SEVEN

"Are you sure you don't want to wear a costume for Halloween?" Olivia asks. "I can let you borrow my hat."

I'm sitting on Olivia's bed as she looks at all the angles of her black dress in the full-length mirror. Olivia is a very convincing witch. The sleeves and hem look wind-torn from broom rides. Her makeup is dark and spooky, and she's applied bloodred lipstick for the full dramatic effect.

Jasmine has invited her to a Halloween dinner party. When Olivia asked if I wanted to come too, I told her I wanted to go trick-or-treating in the neighborhood.

I haven't gone trick-or-treating since I left Boston. For the last two years, Olivia and I stayed in the RV and watched scary movies. When I was little, my father would take me trick-or-treating in our apartment building. One year I wore a fairy costume, and a group of women gushed over me. They were all dressed for some fancy party—feathered hats, shiny jewelry, and satin gowns. Their pale hands adjusted the glittery wings Olivia had made for me. But I couldn't tell my father about Tilly, Cleo, and Dawn because I already knew he couldn't see them. The air was full of buzzy excitement as the dead mingled with each other, all of them smiling knowingly at me. The ghosts knew I was more than a believer—they knew I had a special gift. This is when I realized Halloween was a night for ghosts to come out of hiding. There were so many just in my apartment building. After that night, I looked forward to every Halloween and reuniting with the dead.

Tonight, the Dead Club would reunite with Violet.

"I don't feel like wearing a costume," I say as I adjust my hoodie. "I want to be comfortable."

Olivia approaches me and touches my freshly installed braids—my latest choice is a dark purple bundle I bought at the beauty supply store.

"Hate to break it to you, but you're going to need to put in more effort," Olivia says. "This neighborhood takes Halloween very seriously, and if you don't look like you have on some type of costume, you're going to get dusty gum. None of the good stuff, and I personally want you to bring me back some full-size Snickers bars."

She reaches for her witch hat and pushes it into my chest. The club does plan to go trick-or-treating, so I take the hat and let Olivia make my face look spooky like hers. When she's done, she inspects her work.

"Now you look like a soccer mom witch," she laughs.

When the doorbell rings, I jump off the bed. "That's Miki and Danni-Lynn coming to get me."

When I get to the staircase, I can already hear their

voices inside the house, and I'm confused until I see the girls in the open doorway with Jasmine.

"I let your little club friends in," she says. "I was right behind them."

Jasmine is also dressed up as a witch, but she has on a long platinum wig, a short red dress with fishnet stockings, and battered combat boots. Lincoln trots up to the porch and into the house. He's painted his face green and wears jeans and a ripped oxford shirt.

"What are you supposed to be?" I ask.

Lincoln laughs. "You don't know? I'm Skinny Hulk."

Danni-Lynn giggles as he flexes his nonexistent muscles. "You *are* skinny."

The girls are dressed like me, and they've also made a half-hearted attempt in their Halloween costumes. I didn't know Danni-Lynn even owned a pair of jeans. She has on a fancy tiara, and instead of her string of pearls, she wears a rhinestone necklace. It's easy to guess she's a princess. But I'm at a loss for what Miki is supposed to be—she's wearing a fake mustache and a unicorn headband.

Jasmine examines each of us. "These are interesting costume choices."

"The verdict is still out if they'll get any good candy," Olivia says as she comes down the staircase.

Jasmine squeals at Olivia's costume and commands Lincoln to take several photos. Olivia grabs me for poses and she does the same with Danni-Lynn and Miki. After our photo session is over, we all go outside on the porch.

"Remember, you have to be back here at nine p.m. No excuses," Olivia tells me. "Even if I'm late getting home, I'll be able to tell by the tracker on your phone if you're not here."

We follow the two witches and Skinny Hulk to the gate. In the twilight, several younger kids pass us on the sidewalk. Some wear superhero capes while others have on clown and pirate costumes. A kid dressed as a vampire with glow-in-the-dark fangs skips by us too. All their bags are already full of candy.

Danni-Lynn waves at Olivia and Jasmine as they get into Lincoln's car at the curb. When they drive away, Miki lets out a relieved sigh.

"Let's get this ghost-hunting party started." She pulls out her flashlight.

The Leehans don't have their porch light on, so the house lies in shadows. Miki raises her flashlight and presses the button to perform a beaming pattern that shines into the upstairs window. The lamp turns on, repeating the same pattern as a response.

We wait at the gate and my body swells with nerves. Danni-Lynn grabs Miki's hand, and the girls move closer together. They've waited so long to see their friend again.

A dark figure emerges from the porch. It stops in the shadows before moving into the yard and then into the street.

Although Violet has on overall shorts, she doesn't look out of place because the air isn't cold tonight. A group of trick-or-treaters moves around her—proof that believers seeing the dead on Halloween is real.

Miki and Danni-Lynn are both believers too. Can they see the ghost? A heartbeat passes before I get my answer.

Miki sprints into the street and crashes into Violet. Surprised, the ghost moves slowly at first, but then her arms quickly wrap tight around Miki's trembling shoulders.

I've had interactions with the dead, but nothing this intense. Tilly, Cleo, and Dawn squealed about my Halloween costumes and gave me cold kisses. But since then, the only ghosts I've met were looking for answers. Now seeing the tearful reunion between Miki and Violet, I wonder if the power of a heartfelt hug is what some of those ghosts needed.

Danni-Lynn slowly approaches the two girls in the street and soon she's brought into their embrace. I remain at the gate, and watch the reunited best friends laugh and wipe happy tears from each other's faces.

When the girls part, Violet moves forward to greet me. "Hi, Wednesday."

"I'm glad to see you again," I tell her.

She looks at Nana's house. "Have you talked to Caleb?"

"No, but if we bring the wicked ghost inside the house, he'll take care of it."

Danni-Lynn comes to stand next to me. "Did Wednesday tell you she wants to lure the bad ghost by using herself as bait? For the record, I think it's a bad idea."

Miki joins us at the gate. "First, we have to find it, or

at least get its attention. Violet, do you have any ideas of where we can start looking?"

"We don't even know if it's still interested in Wednesday," Danni-Lynn says.

"Maybe it's been waiting for Halloween to make its move," Violet says. "That's when it attacked me."

"If that's the case, then we won't have to hunt it at all. That thing will find us before we find it." Miki frowns at the possibility.

"It could be anywhere, y'all!" Danni-Lynn protests. "What if it's not in the neighborhood anymore?"

"Laura Tarkington didn't show up again today in the cafeteria, so she's still hiding," I remind her. "And Violet's right. Halloween *is* different. This night can make ghosts bold—especially the wicked ones. The best-case scenario is that it's gone, but we should still take a look around. If it's here, we need to banish it once and for all."

CHAPTER TWENTY-EIGHT

My trick-or-treat bag is heavy with full-size chocolate bars, packs of gummy worms, and different kinds of lollipops. Olivia was right about giving me the witch hat and doing my spooky makeup—no one has given me stale gum yet.

As we walk through the neighborhood, Violet points to all the houses that are haunted. I can tell by the gleam in her eyes, she's just as fascinated by the dead as she was when she was alive.

"I didn't realize how many ghosts were here until I became one," Violet says, her voice now serious.

The truth is we all end up as ghosts in the end, and no one is ever ready. I've learned that fact enough times dealing with the dead and their unfinished business. No one is done with living when the time comes.

"I never told you what I found about your parents," I tell Violet. "Do you want to know where they are now?"

She glances at me and then slowly nods. When I reveal that her parents are living in Miami with her baby brother, she gives me a bittersweet smile. "I knew they left . . . but I was so worried about them. It's good to know they're doing okay." Violet pauses, and then her face fills with delight. "I've always wanted to be a big sister."

Danni-Lynn adjusts her tiara as she trots up next to us. "If the bad ghost can steal faces, how will we know that we've found it? What exactly should we be looking for, anyway?"

Miki squeezes in between me and Violet. "Good question."

"When I saw it last Halloween, I thought it was a lost kid, but then it changed into a creepy corpse," Violet says. "It doesn't seem to be able to keep a disguise for long."

I shudder and push the memories of the dark Arizona forest away. "Violet is right. Wicked ghosts can't keep their stolen form for a long period of time. It has to show its true form sooner than later."

"Great." Danni-Lynn grimaces in disgust. "Sorry I asked."

"We need to look out for anyone who's taken an interest in us," I tell them. "Or someone who has on a gory costume that looks way *too good* to be fake."

We continue to trick-or-treat, but after walking the neighborhood grid, there's no sign of anything wicked. No suspicious ghost is following us. The ones who do cross our path are too busy with their own agendas. The dark clouds in my brain have stopped stirring, and I try to keep the tiny seed of hope from growing in my chest, but now it's starting to take root.

Maybe the wicked ghost is gone.

We decide to travel to Hampshire Avenue and pass Miki's house, then turn right onto Sinclair Street. We hear the noise before we see the house. Several people are out on the lawn. Most of them are older kids, but I recognize a few of our classmates. A group of adults are huddled at the side of the house having their own party. Orange floodlights and Halloween decorations hang from the trees.

Violet leans over the hedges and gawks at the festivities. "Sunny Trafford is having a Halloween party?"

"We weren't invited, so who cares," Miki sneers.

Danni-Lynn moves closer to Violet. "Sunny is on the spirit squad, so Alexa is probably here."

Violet gives Danni-Lynn a mischievous look. "Let's crash it!"

Miki and I follow behind them as they prance into the party like they belong there. The boom of the music echoes in my chest. Violet's face is full of excitement as she looks around. Danni-Lynn bats her eyes at several boys while Miki gives them angry glares.

As we move through the crowd, the same group of girls I saw at the Beloved Bakery are gathered in a tight circle. When they notice me, they whisper and point in my direction, but Danni-Lynn's cousin, Audrey Abbott, ignores us.

"They're not worth our energy," Danni-Lynn tells me. "Especially not tonight."

We find Alexa on the porch. She's with Sunny and a few other girls from the spirit squad. Instead of wearing a costume, Alexa has on a sparkly top that shimmers on her dark brown skin. Her hair is up in one large, cottony puff. When she sees the four of us, a cup of punch falls from her hand and splatters everywhere.

One of the spirit squad girls veers quickly away and shrieks. "Alexa! You almost *ruined* my shoes!"

Alexa ignores the girl and quickly moves down the porch steps to meet us. She stares at Violet in awe.

"I—I . . ." She stops talking when Sunny appears by her side. She's also wearing a shiny top, and her blond hair falls loose around her shoulders.

"Are you okay, Alexa?" Sunny asks. "You acted like you saw a ghost."

When Sunny doesn't get an answer, she turns and squints at me. Slowly, a faint recognition appears on her face.

"Hey, you're that girl Wendy who freaked out in the cafeteria a few weeks ago."

"Her name is *Wednesday*," Miki corrects her. "And she didn't freak out, she *actually* saw a gh—"

"This is such a good party, Sunny," Danni-Lynn interrupts Miki. "I think my invitation may have gotten lost? Anyway, I'm so happy I could stop by and say hello."

Sunny should remember Violet, but she doesn't notice her at all. She must not be a believer, so she can't see the dead on Halloween. But Alexa's gaze is still locked on Violet.

When she blinks, her bottom lip quivers, and I'm afraid she's about to cry. I know Alexa can't talk to Violet at this party—not in front of Sunny and the rest of her friends.

I quickly move in front of her. "Alexa, I'm glad we found you."

Miki glances at me before she takes Violet's hand. "We'll go and wait on the sidewalk."

"Alexa, if you want to talk, come find us," Danni-Lynn tells her.

I follow the girls as they weave through the party. When I look back, Alexa hasn't moved. Sunny whispers in her ear before she returns to the porch.

Out on the sidewalk, we wait a few minutes, but it doesn't take long for Alexa to rush out of the party, frantically searching for Violet. Her eyes are full of disbelief as she approaches us.

"It's really me this time." Violet smiles at her.

"I thought I would never see you again," Alexa says.

This reunion is different from the one Violet had with Danni-Lynn and Miki. Gentle and quiet, but just as strong. The two girls whisper to each other and repair their broken bond from the wicked ghost. Even if it's just on this night, Alexa can see Violet without her gift.

When they pull apart, Alexa turns to the rest of us. "Y'all went trick-or-treating?"

"That's our cover." Miki winces as she pulls off her mustache. "We're actually looking for the wicked ghost."

Alexa shakes her head. "You know that's not a good idea."

"That's what I said too, Alexa!" Danni-Lynn says.

"Listen, y'all. We should all go to Miki's house and watch the *Loveburned* Halloween episode."

I pull out my phone from my hoodie pocket. It's only 8:15 p.m. We still have some time left before my curfew.

"Let's go to the park," I tell them. "Maybe the school ghosts have come out of hiding, and we can ask Laura Tarkington about the wicked ghost. She may know where it is."

"We do need to cover all our bases," Violet agrees. "Make sure it isn't roaming around there."

"Fine." Danni-Lynn crosses her arms. "We can go to the park, but after that, we should let this ghost chase go, because it's really working my nerves."

"I promise if we can't find it, we'll all go home." I turn to Alexa. "We'll see you later, okay?"

"I don't think so." She narrows her eyes at me. "I'm coming with y'all."

CHAPTER TWENTY-NINE

On the way to the park, we pass a woman in a housecoat talking to a man in an army uniform. When they pass, the whiff of cold that moves over my skin tells me they aren't wearing costumes. The ghosts don't pay me any attention. I nudge Alexa and tilt my head toward them.

"They've been walking up and down Sinclair Street all night," she tells me. "It's weird seeing so many ghosts when I haven't been able to see any at all."

When we make our way to the park, the annual neighborhood Fall Festival is winding down, and several vendors have already started to dismantle their stalls.

Violet keeps walking through the park, and we follow her until we're standing in the courtyard of Noble Middle School. Two boys dressed as skeletons are playing a mini game of soccer, and a girl dressed as an angel sits on the grass and watches them. Bright floodlights keep the shadow of night away, and there's no sign of the wicked ghost lurking near the school.

We sit at one of the stone tables. Miki empties her trick-or-treat bag and begins to organize her candy.

"You know you can do that when you get home," Alexa says.

"It's giving me something to do," Miki tells her.

When I turn to ask Violet a question, she's no longer at the table with us. I search the courtyard to see if she's there, but the ghost has disappeared. I notice the angel girl and the skeleton boys are also gone. A cold tingle brushes against my neck.

"Where's Violet?" Danni-Lynn asks.

"The kids in the courtyard are gone too." My heartbeat is fast and loud in my ears.

Alexa's eyes grow wide. "They were ghosts?! They looked—"

"I didn't know they were dead either," I tell her. "That's the thing about Halloween—you can't tell unless you're close enough to feel the cold."

"What do we do now?" Alexa says.

Danni-Lynn looks at the empty courtyard and cuts her eyes back to me. "Should we leave?"

We sit and stare at each other for a moment, and then we all jump when the alarm on my phone goes off. I have fifteen minutes left until Olivia's curfew.

"Wednesday, maybe you should get back to your house, where it's safe," Alexa suggests.

"Now that's the best idea I've heard all night." Danni-Lynn helps Miki put all her candy back in her bag.

We move through the courtyard to the park and find Violet talking to Laura Tarkington. Both ghosts quickly motion us to join them.

"We thought you left us!" Miki's voice cracks.

Laura Tarkington is still wearing her yellow peacoat,

and the blood on the hem of her dress is dark in the dim light. The guide ghost doesn't look scared like the last time I saw her.

"Hi, Wednesday." Her face is kind, and she smiles at me. "Sorry I've haven't been around."

"It's okay," I tell her.

The coldness around me is stronger, and I take a closer look at the kids and adults. Most of their clothes are modern, but others seem from an earlier time. When I spot the two skeleton boys and the angel girl, I realize all these people are ghosts.

"I asked, but no one has seen the wicked ghost," Violet says. "And it's stolen most of our faces here, so I don't think it's interested in any of us tonight."

"We believe it's gone." Laura Tarkington comes to stand between me and Alexa. "That's why we've come out of hiding."

I scan the darkening park, relief spreading over my skin. I've been afraid of what could happen—what could go wrong. But I also feel a twinge of disappointment. If the wicked ghost is gone, that means it's found a living host—and another life has been stolen.

The alarm on my phone goes off again. Five minutes left until Olivia's curfew.

"I need to go," I tell everyone.

"We'll follow you back to your house," Laura Tarkington says as she motions the other ghosts to follow her.

The neighborhood is now nestling into its usual night

sounds along with the low buzzing of the lampposts. Most of the porch lights are now turned off, a signal to the straggling trick-or-treaters that the time of free candy is over.

Laura Tarkington moves ahead of us, but then veers off the sidewalk away from the lampposts. I slow down my pace as a bolt of lightning strikes in my brain—a warning. I turn and look back at Violet, who's talking with Miki.

Alexa moves closer to me. "What's she doing?"

The woman in the yellow peacoat walks into the street, opens her arms wide, and laughs.

Alexa grabs my hand as the ghost moves in jerky motions. Laura Tarkington's face changes, no longer pale and flushed pink from a winter day. Her features and form flicker. Different ghosts appear in front of me. A girl with angel wings. A boy in a skeleton costume. A man in an army uniform. Then Violet's face stares at me, giving me a devious grin.

The wicked ghost morphs into several other versions of the dead—until it reveals another form, different from the rest. Scraps of dirty cloth cling to its skeletal body—not even rotting flesh remains on the bones. This is its true form.

"I've been watching you, Wednesday." Its voice is evil and menacing. "Talking to you with *two* different faces."

Violet moves in front of me. Her hands are balled tight into fists. She's angry and determined, and I wonder if she protected her friends as fiercely as this when she was alive.

"You don't belong here," Violet says.

"I *do* belong here, and I am going to *stay* here." The wicked ghost turns its gaze on Alexa. "I thought it might be you. Your gift was strong, but I felt weakness in you, and later you proved to me that I was right."

"You're not going to hurt anyone here," Violet tells the wicked ghost.

"I am not afraid of you." The decayed form cackles. "You are wretched and weak. No different from the others here."

The wicked ghost changes again, scattering apart into slivers of darkness. I gape at this familiar form—I witnessed the same transformation in the Arizona forest right before my possession.

"I was going to leave this pathetic place," a voice says above us. "After scouring that school for months, I never found the right body, the right life. Then you arrived, Wednesday, with the strongest gift I have seen in years."

Violet pushes me toward Nana's house. "Run, Wednesday! Let it follow you! *Now!*"

I pump my legs as I pound the pavement. I'm not sure where the wicked ghost is—whether it's behind or above me. But if I lead it to Nana's house in its current form, I know the wicked ghost will follow me.

I sprint down the sidewalk, and Nana's pale yellow house appears. I'm going to make it. I'm going to rush up the porch steps. I'm going to leap inside to safety.

But as I run, Nana's house doesn't get closer—my arms and legs feel like deadweights. A sharp pain twists in my chest, and a wave of nausea hits me.

It's happening again.

I try to push the air out of my lungs but the pressure increases, and I feel like I'm being dragged underneath a stormy ocean. I try to take another breath, but it only pushes me deeper under the waves.

The brightness of my Lodestar explodes around me—a beacon of my own protection. If I follow this light, the wicked ghost won't find my soul. I'll leave my body and only return when the evil has uncoiled from around my heart.

I've made it to the gate. I'm so close to Nana's house. If the wicked ghost follows me inside, Caleb will sense its presence. He'll banish it, and then it won't be able to torment the living or the dead anymore.

I'm too close to fail now.

The light of my Lodestar dims as I open the gate and stumble through the yard. My vision collapses into a pinprick of light, and the world around me turns pitch-black. Frantic voices surround me as my legs leave the ground.

A voice enters my head—ancient and devious.

"I am glad that I was patient with you," it says. "So, so very patient. Do you want to know why I waited until tonight? I wanted to see if your power would dim like all the others. Your gifted soul will be useful to me as I live in this body."

A hard shove slams me down into darkness—a closed coffin under six feet of dirt. I let out a scream, but I already know no one can hear me.

CHAPTER THIRTY

The darkness slowly peels away, and I'm in my room. But not the room in Nana's house. It's my old room in Boston, where I lived with my parents before they broke up.

My favorite stuffed bunny and giraffe huddle around me on the canopy bed. Drawings of rainbows, trees, and butterflies are taped to the walls. Happy memories flood me with such force that tears spring to my eyes. I loved this room.

Outside, a winter storm churns snow into drifts as tall as mountains. When I open the window and let the blizzard into my room, I smile as the snowflakes feel like warm sugar on my skin.

I step out to the fire escape and search for the familiar skyline of my childhood, but it's not there. Instead, in the distance, the snow disappears into the edges of a desert swirling under a blue sky with two blazing suns. I stare in wonder at a caravan of ant-size travelers walking across the sand. I turn in the other direction, and a sea churns under a night sky full of stars. Tiny boats with white sails float toward the horizon. The desert and the sea seem vast, like different universes—beautiful and eternal.

When I return to my room, I open the door and find a hallway filled with people wearing fancy clothes. Loud music fills the air as I walk through the dancing crowd.

A hand gently touches my shoulder, and I turn to see three women dressed in feathered hats and satin gowns. Tilly, Cleo, and Dawn—the ghosts who would visit me every Halloween.

"Where's your costume, Wednesday?" Dawn asks.

"I don't remember you being so tall," Tilly says.

"Why do you look so sad?" Cleo touches my face. "This is a party!"

"I—I don't understand," I stutter. "What are you doing here?"

The women look at each other and laugh, which makes the other ghosts around them laugh too.

"Honey, you *summoned* us," Dawn says.

"Tell us what you want, love." Tilly leans close to me. "Do you need to talk to someone on this side?"

The hairs on the back of my neck stand up because I realize my Lodestar has brought me to the spirit realm. Tilly, Cleo, and Dawn must have crossed over after I left Boston. I stare at the women's pale, cheerful faces. The party rumbles around us as the other ghosts sing and dance.

"I'm looking for my great-grandmother," I say. "She died eleven years ago."

"Ah, Wednesday is looking for family!" Cleo claps gleefully at my response. "What's her name?"

"Josephine Marlow," I tell her.

"She won't be at this party, Wednesday." Tilly takes my hand. "We'll have to go look for her."

"How will you know where to find her?" I ask.

The women exchange uneasy glances, and I wonder if it's possible for them to locate Nana in the spirit realm.

Cleo releases a nervous, lighthearted laugh. "Let us worry about that, Wednesday."

The three women guide me to my room and tuck me into bed. Each of them gives me a warm kiss on my forehead.

"We'll be back soon," Dawn promises me.

When the door closes, a sense of calm stirs inside me. Now that my soul is in the spirit realm, Nana will come help me.

I don't know how much time has passed when I blink awake. I'm cozy and warm in my bed, and the snow is still falling outside. But my room has changed. The walls are bare, and my stuffed animals are gone too. Frowning, I get up and open the door.

Instead of seeing a crowded hallway full of festive ghosts, there's a brick wall. I touch the cold, rough surface and then bang against it. When I yell, no one answers me.

Anxious thoughts fill my brain. Tilly, Cleo, and Dawn couldn't find Nana. Now what will happen to me? How long can my soul stay here?

I try to fight the growing fear about what's happening

on the other side. I don't know if the Dead Club got me inside Nana's house or if they found Caleb. But I want to keep believing my friends are doing their best to help me, and I should do the same thing for myself here in the spirit realm.

This time when I open the window, the cold bites at my skin and icicles form on my lashes. I take a deep breath, and sharp frost coats my throat.

I was thinking about the three ghosts from my childhood before I came to the spirit realm. Maybe that's why the women appeared to me—they felt my presence. Maybe summoning the dead is the same as setting an intention. Maybe this is what I need to do to summon Nana.

Trembling in the cold, I close my eyes and focus on my great-grandmother. I remember the stories Olivia has told me about Nana's wisdom and kindness. I visualize her appearance from old photos—an elderly woman in devout black.

"Nana, can you hear me?" I whisper. "It's Wednesday."

I open my eyes as the snow whirls in response. In the distance, several shadows glide toward me. But as they get closer, they veer in opposite directions. Some go to the desert with the blazing suns while others venture toward the sea under the night sky. Although the snow is heavy and wet on my braids, I wait for Nana to answer my call.

But no other shadows come to greet me.

A low dread fills my chest. If the spirit realm does contain vast universes, Nana could be anywhere. Too far away to hear me. Too far away to save me.

"You're not a baby anymore," a voice behind me says.

When I turn around, there's an elderly woman in my room. The same one I've imagined from memories and stories. When my great-grandmother smiles at me, I rush into her arms.

"I heard you, Wednesday," Nana whispers in my ear.

But our joy is short-lived. Now my canopy bed is gone, and the colors of my room have faded to a grayish gloom.

Nana notices my distress and squeezes my shoulder. "Your Lodestar is weakening, which means your time in the spirit realm will be over soon. Tell me why you're here."

Her brown eyes are gentle and patient as she listens to me. By the time I'm done, the room has grown darker.

"Can you help me, Nana?"

"If your body is in the house, then it's safe," she says. "Those girls will get you to Caleb, and he'll take care of that wicked spirit."

A slow realization comes to me. When Nana used her Lodestar to come here, she summoned ghosts to get information for her patrons. These ghosts couldn't interfere with what happened on the other side. In the spirit realm, Nana doesn't have the power to banish the wicked ghost. She can't help me.

I swallow panic as a new storm surges in my brain. What will happen to me when my Lodestar dims away? Will my soul go back to the terrifying darkness of the wicked ghost's prison?

The floor shakes beneath us, and Nana squeezes my

shoulder again. My room returns to its original form with my bed, stuffed animals, and taped drawings on the wall. But then it flickers back to the empty, gray shell. Whatever is happening on the other side also has a ripple effect here in my Lodestar. A few moments later, the frantic voices of my friends echo around the room. Nana cocks her head as she listens too.

"I was much older than you when I first arrived in the spirit realm," she says. "Caleb could use a Lodestar at your age, but he couldn't sense what was happening on the other side like you can. This is something very rare, Wednesday. You may be the strongest descendant of our family yet."

"Is there anything I can do?" I ask.

Nana examines me closely before she speaks. "Caleb is on the other side with your body while your soul is here. If you can form a bond with him, then maybe *you* can banish the wicked spirit."

The Callahan House, October 31, 9:07 p.m.

On Noble Avenue, in the haunted house across the street, Violet Delgado searches for the Callahan ghost.

Panic-filled yells surround her as the other Dead Club members drag their possessed medium inside. Violet has already searched the other rooms on the first floor, but she's found no sign of Caleb Callahan. She peers up the dark staircase and wonders if the ghost could be lurking on the second floor.

Violet wants to be scared, but the stillness in her chest doesn't create the emotion of fear. There's no heartbeat to push blood through her veins. She hasn't felt anything since she died. Her body is now a hollow box, empty of physical reactions. Only faint memories of emotions haunt her now.

"Where's Caleb?" one of the girls shouts at her. "We need his help!"

"Let me keep looking for him," Violet says as she bolts up the staircase.

Alexa Scott carries the medium by her arms while the other two club members hold each of the girl's legs. They stumble into the den and put her on the sofa.

The medium's eyelids flutter, but Wednesday Thomas

isn't dreaming. The wicked ghost is now slithering under her skin toward her chest so it can coil around her heart.

"What do we do now?"

Alexa switches her gaze from the medium to the Dead Club's new president. Miki Okada's eyes are full of fright. She saw the wicked ghost scatter into dark slivers and overtake Wednesday's body. On any other night, Miki wouldn't have seen the dead at all, but as a believer on Halloween, she witnessed Wednesday's terrifying possession.

Miki hovers over the club's medium, wringing her hands. "Should we call 911?"

Only Wednesday's shallow breathing reveals that she may be unwell. Inside her body, the wicked ghost searches for the girl's soul, but the medium is no longer on this physical plane.

"A hospital can't fix this," Alexa says.

"Should we call her mom?" Miki suggests.

The Dead Club's secretary and historian, Danni-Lynn Porter, sits on the sofa and gently places Wednesday's head into her lap. She doesn't like how the raw cold seeps through her clothes as if the medium is made of ice.

"Her mama will be here soon enough," Danni-Lynn says. "She'll know what to do."

At first, Danni-Lynn was glad that the house was empty. The last thing she wants is to get into trouble, but she now hopes Wednesday's mother comes home soon.

"What if Caleb isn't in the house?" Miki asks.

"He's here, and Violet will find him," Alexa says.

"But what if she *can't* find him?" Miki's face flushes with worry. "It's Halloween! What if he left?"

"Violet will find him," Alexa repeats, more for herself than for Miki.

Upstairs, Violet searches for the Callahan ghost, but finds all the rooms empty. She remembers how frustration bunched in her shoulders and made her neck warm as she swiftly ascends the narrow stairs to the turret.

Moving through the small room full of art supplies and unfinished easels, Violet checks under tables and opens closet doors. She doesn't understand that searching for the dead isn't the same as searching for the living. On this plane, ghosts use their free will to decide when to appear, even to their own kind. But Caleb isn't hiding from Violet. He's already sensed the wicked ghost in the house.

Downstairs, the temperature in the den has changed. The chill gives Alexa the same jolt as it did when she was a little girl and saw her first ghost. She rises from the sofa and moves toward the cold spot.

Miki follows Alexa to the den's open sliding doors, and she shivers as her breath releases cloudy puffs into the air. Footsteps descend the staircase, and both girls move forward to see if the Callahan ghost has finally come to save their medium. But it's only Violet who meets them.

"I can't find Caleb," she says. "I've looked everywhere."

Danni-Lynn's scream alerts them, and they all scramble into the den. With her hand over her mouth, Danni-Lynn points toward a small, fragile boy in pajamas.

Caleb stares at Wednesday on the sofa, and although

memories are different in death, he remembers Wednesday is Josephine Marlow's great-granddaughter. He showed her the bound ghost across the street. The same one who is here now.

"Is that him?" Miki whispers.

Violet has only seen Caleb in old photographs, and she gapes at his sunken cheeks and the dark bruise around his neck. She doesn't understand that his appearance is also a choice of his free will. Before Violet can ask Caleb for help, his voice enters her mind.

You need to hold Wednesday still.

She quickly looks at the others, but she knows they haven't heard the ghost.

"We—we need to hold Wednesday down for Caleb," Violet says.

"What? How do you know that?" Alexa asks.

Miki rushes to the sofa and wraps her arms around Wednesday's legs, but Alexa remains next to Violet, baffled at the instructions.

"I can hear him in my head," Violet tells her.

"You mean like ghost telepathy?"

"I guess so? I don't understand how it works, but we need to do what he says."

The choking had taken Caleb's ability to speak, and it followed him in death. Caleb prefers to communicate this way, if he chooses to communicate at all.

I know what is here. It will take all of you to keep Wednesday still for me.

"Caleb says he needs all of us to hold her down."

Violet moves forward and grips Wednesday's arms.

Alexa follows Violet to the sofa and braces Wednesday's hips. Danni-Lynn holds tight onto the medium's shoulders, but then she lets out a gasp.

"Y'all, something is wrong."

Wednesday's eyes have opened, and they glow solid white in the low-lit room. The medium hasn't returned to her body, but the wicked ghost coiled around her heart has sensed a threat.

"Is she having a seizure?" Miki presses harder on Wednesday's legs. "Maybe we *should* call 911."

"No, we have to do what Caleb told us," Alexa says.

The Callahan ghost slowly approaches the sofa. His face is calm, but there's a dangerous hunger in the curve of his smile. Violet remembers how her body reacted to terror, and how the hairs would rise up on the back of her neck. Although her body can no longer process these physical reactions, there's enough phantom memory to conjure a small shudder.

Danni-Lynn clutches Wednesday's shoulders, but the wicked ghost still lifts the medium's body off the sofa. The others hold firm to Wednesday's hips, legs, and arms, and together they push her back onto the sofa's cushions.

Caleb hovers over the medium and smiles wider. The rot that he senses tells him that this wicked ghost is older than the dead woman who came for him, older than what had possessed the little girl, and older than all the others who've crossed the threshold to his grandfather's house.

Keep Wednesday still, and I will be done soon.

Violet tells the Dead Club to keep doing their best to hold Wednesday down for the banishment, and they all watch as the Callahan ghost puts his small, frail hand over Wednesday's heart.

Unlike Violet, Caleb can feel emotion in his body, and he uses anger as his weapon. Helplessly, he watched the dead woman who possessed his father take away his family. When the rage followed him in death, he devoured the dead woman and purged her wretched soul for her cruelty. Caleb stewed in his fury and terrorized the living until Josephine Marlow moved into his grandfather's house.

Now Caleb's hand rests on the home of Wednesday's soul. He knows the wicked ghost that has possessed her has sensed his presence, but it won't be a match for his righteous anger.

When the wicked ghost loosens its grip around Wednesday's heart, Caleb's hunger grows. He wants to purge the rotten soul and devour it like all the others until nothing is left but a horrid, fading stain.

Caleb's anticipation grows as the wicked ghost dislodges from around Wednesday's heart. Her breathing grows shallow, and Caleb leans forward. He waits eagerly for the rot to expel from her body.

The medium's mouth opens, and a horrendous stench fills the air. Caleb moves closer and quickly grabs a slick, wet tentacle that unfurls from between Wednesday's lips. Now expelled against its will, the wicked ghost is seeking escape. Caleb pulls at the writhing form, ignoring the disgusted cries from the others around him.

His hunger grows as he continues to tug at the rotting menace. He opens his mouth, craving to devour the wicked ghost's dark energy into his body and then purge it from this physical plane.

He frowns as the wiggling form grows warm in his hands. In a forceful shake, the slick, mottled tentacle jerks away from his grip and retreats into Wednesday's body.

Stricken with surprise, Caleb senses the wicked ghost coil and constrict around the medium's heart again.

"What happened?" Violet asks him. "Did something go wrong?"

Although time has no meaning for Caleb, the moment stretches with this new experience in death. The voices of the others fill the room with desperate questions and rising shouts, but the Callahan ghost doesn't have any answers. He has failed to banish the wicked ghost. Before this hopeless fear can overwhelm him, his fingers tingle with warmth, and a voice enters his mind.

Caleb, can you hear me? It's Wednesday.

Caleb jerks his hand away from the medium's chest. He looks toward the others, but he knows that they haven't heard Wednesday's voice. The medium's soul has reached across life and death to speak only to him.

The lights flicker in the den, and Wednesday's eyes open again, but her eyes are now brown. The wicked ghost spits out a sordid cackle.

"You cannot take me against my will," the wicked ghost taunts them using the medium's voice. "This is my body now. *My gift.*"

Violet narrows her eyes in determination and presses harder on Wednesday's arms. Miki, Alexa, and Danni-Lynn follow her lead and keep holding the medium down on the sofa.

"Don't listen to it, Caleb," Violet says. "Try again. Please! We can't give up now."

The anger rises sharply in the Callahan ghost as he returns his palm over Wednesday's heart. An anguished cry unleashes from Wednesday's throat and worm-like cords move under her skin. The lights in the den flicker again as the medium convulses. Caleb senses the wicked ghost's retreat, and he waits hungrily to pull the ghost's damp carcass out of Wednesday's mouth.

When the medium's body stops struggling and finally falls limp, Caleb feels nothing but a baffling emptiness underneath his palm.

Miki and Alexa frantically try to shake Wednesday awake but get no response, and Danni-Lynn cries out in fear.

"Y'all, she's not moving!" Danni-Lynn cradles the medium's head in her arms. "Wednesday, wake up!"

Confusion overtakes Caleb until a figure appears, surrounded by light. Wednesday is standing in a doorway, but she's not in his grandfather's house. The doorway isn't on this physical plane. The room brightens around him as the medium speaks to him.

Caleb, I've pulled the wicked ghost into the spirit realm. Let me banish it.

Violet watches the other ghost closely as he stares at the den's open sliding doors. She turns to look, but she only sees empty space. When Violet studies Caleb's face again, it's not full of alarm but of acceptance.

"What did you see?" she whispers to him.

Violet feels a shift in her body after Caleb's answer swirls in her mind. This emotion doesn't match any of her faint memories. It's a new feeling, a swift certainty.

"What did Caleb say to you?" Miki asks.

Violet turns to her best friend as the unnamed emotion continues to fill up the hollow box inside her, overwhelming all her other muted senses of sadness, anger, and loneliness.

"Wednesday . . . she pulled the wicked ghost to the other side. That's . . . that's where she is. She told Caleb that she was going to banish it herself."

"What if she doesn't come back?" Danni-Lynn's tearful voice shakes. "What if she never wakes up?"

"We have to trust Wednesday," Alexa says. "She'll come back to us."

Caleb moves away from the others as new emotions burn inside him. The anger and hunger have leached from his body, breaking his long fever. He feels the weariness of his past rage, but that burden softens into relief. Then soon afterward, a profound yearning rises in him.

When Violet joins him by the fireplace, she wonders if

he's struggling with the same intense emotion that burns inside her. Caleb doesn't wait for her to ask the question.

What you feel is a calling from the other side. Your unfinished business will be done soon too.

After hearing Caleb's voice in her mind, Violet nods solemnly at his truth and understands that her soul wants to leave this physical plane. With no other business to take care of on this side, the longing will tear her apart if she doesn't cross over to the spirit realm.

For now, Violet will endure this emotional turmoil and wait until Wednesday's soul returns to her body.

CHAPTER THIRTY-ONE

My Lodestar trembles and the ceiling opens like the lid of a box. Dark clouds gather and low thunder announces a brewing storm, reminding me of the anxiety I felt in my brain—all the fear and worry from my experiences with the dead.

"How do I form a bond with Caleb?" I ask Nana.

"This is your Lodestar, baby," she says. "You'll need to determine how to connect with him."

The clouds above us grow darker, and the floor shakes. A sharp pain erupts in my chest, and the agony is unbearable until I put my hand over my heart. The ache dulls to a pulse, but not like a heartbeat. My body is still on the other side.

Heat tingles under my hand, and a wave of certainty washes over me—an inner knowing. Summoning is an intention in the spirit realm, and now I realize it can work on the other side too.

I close my eyes and focus on the Callahan ghost. Caleb's fragile body and sad eyes. The bruise around his neck. I visualize Nana's house, with its gable roof and windows. The black iron gate. My warm fingertips grow hot, and I push out my intention from my heart.

"Caleb, can you hear me? It's Wednesday."

The floor rumbles in response, and I open my eyes. A bright light shines through the cracks of my bedroom door. When I open it, the brick wall is gone, and my room brightens with a radiant glow. Tiny specks float in the air like cosmic dust and shimmer on my skin.

Nana's house is beyond the doorway. My body is lying on the sofa in the den, surrounded by the Dead Club. The Callahan ghost is leaning over me with his hand over my heart. The lights in the den flicker, and the girls frantically press down on my arms, legs, and shoulders.

Another sharp pain erupts in my chest, and I let out a loud gasp. In Nana's house, my body jerks and convulses.

"What do you see, Wednesday?" Nana asks.

"I can see the house. The girls have found Caleb, and he's trying to banish the wicked ghost," I tell her. "But . . . something is wrong."

"You've created a bond with him, which means you're connected to the other side."

Caleb hasn't responded to me, but the certainty swells inside me. I put my hand back on my chest, and this time I feel the connection to my body and the darkness lurking inside. The wicked ghost has tightly wrapped itself around my heart, unwilling to let go. I can hear its cackling taunts, and I become angry at its growing pride. The wicked ghost believes it has defeated Caleb. My fingertips grow hot again as I push out another intention.

"You will not steal my life or my gift," I say to the wicked ghost. "Leave my body *now*."

A forceful tug severs the wicked ghost's grip, and a dark mass surges past me into my room. Nana's eyes widen as wet, fleshy tentacles slap against the walls, searching for an escape.

Back at the doorway, Caleb looks up and sees me. When we lock eyes, the confusion on his face turns into understanding.

"Caleb, I've pulled the wicked ghost into the spirit realm. Let me banish it."

Nana's house gradually disappears, and the brick wall returns. I touch the cold, rough surface and know my connection to the other side has ended. Closing the door, I turn to watch the slimy tentacles squirm on the floor and manifest into another form.

The wicked ghost's skeletal body tries to scramble away and find a hiding place. But the manifestation continues as pale flesh covers the wicked ghost's bones and short, dark hair sprouts from its head. Scraps of cloth transform into a toga-like robe.

The spirit realm has revealed the wicked ghost's true identity: a man from an ancient period. He's the oldest ghost I've ever seen, and I've brought him to a place beyond time and space.

"What have you *done*?" he cries as he crumples in defeat on the floor.

When I look at Nana, her face is full of sadness, but she

remains silent as the man continues to tremble with tears.

I don't feel any remorse for bringing this wicked ghost to the afterlife against his will—he tried to steal my life and take my gift as his own. I will never know the amount of suffering this wicked ghost has caused to both the living and the dead. The banishment from the physical plane can't undo all the damage done—but at least now, this ghost can't harm anyone else.

My Lodestar flickers, and the colors of my room drain to lifeless gray. My soul will have to leave the spirit realm soon.

"Your time on the other side is over," I tell the crying man. "You can never go back."

Outside my window, several shadows emerge from the blizzard. Others arrive from the desert and the sea. When they manifest into form, ghosts of different ages and cultures stare blankly at us. When the man senses their presence, he turns to meet their gaze.

A fearful awareness appears on the ghost's face, but there are too many for him to resist. Two men in similar robe-like clothing pull him outside and the other ghosts surround him. Their voices fill the air with a low buzzing hum.

Nana and I watch as the ghosts carry the wailing man away into the white blindness of the blizzard.

"He was so afraid of what came after death that he couldn't perceive that it was only the beginning," Nana quietly tells me. "Now he must make amends to the souls he's harmed. His arrival in the spirit realm summoned them here."

"What will happen to him now?" I ask.

"That's not up to us to decide," Nana says. "But in death, the scales of right and wrong always balance."

The universes outside my window dim and finally disappear. Slowly, my room changes into a colorless, empty space.

"As a living soul, your time in the spirit realm has ended," Nana tells me. "It's time for you to leave."

"But I have so many questions—can I come back here?"

"No need to worry about that now, baby."

I frown in misunderstanding. "But—"

"Your Lodestar brought you here once, so it can bring you back again," Nana says. "I don't know how it will guide you, but I do know it has evolved past the purpose of protection. Now *you* can control how to use it. You'll have to learn how like I did."

I think of the certainty I felt when I connected to the other side and summoned the wicked ghost. If I connect with this inner knowing again, I will find a way to return to the spirit realm.

I reach out for Nana's hands, and they're no longer warm but ice-cold. Nana smiles proudly at me as her form begins to vanish.

"I'll see you again, Wednesday," she says.

After she disappears, I'm alone in the blank void of my

Lodestar. But I'm not afraid. There's no pain or anxiety—only peace.

A gentle tug pulls me upward, and I travel fast through time and space. I'm calm during this journey between life and death. When my speed decreases, I close my eyes and float in the void until I'm pushed into something soft and warm.

My Lodestar has reunited my soul with my body.

CHAPTER THIRTY-TWO

I'm back at Nana's house, lying on the sofa in my hoodie and jeans. Noise arrives in a whoosh of sound.

"Wednesday, you came back!" Danni-Lynn hugs me tightly.

Alexa and Miki stand over me with relieved faces. My chest aches, but the rest of my body doesn't hurt. I wiggle my toes in my sneakers.

When I try to move, Danni-Lynn quickly helps me sit up on the sofa. Across the room, Caleb stands by the fireplace. Violet is beside him, but her face is vacant and lost.

"The wicked ghost is gone," I whisper to them.

Caleb holds my gaze for a moment before he turns to Violet. She furrows her brow as if she's listening to a message that only she can hear. Slowly, she nods in agreement, and then her face falls into sadness.

When Caleb walks past us, his feet are whisper-soft on the floor. A few moments later, the front door opens, and the ghost walks outside. Violet stares longingly at the path Caleb took to leave the house.

Danni-Lynn squeezes my hand. "We were so scared you wouldn't come back."

Alexa sits next to me on the sofa. She tells me how they dragged me inside the house, and I tell them what happened to the wicked ghost in the spirit realm.

Violet moves closer as she listens to me. When I finish, her face is full of deep yearning.

"Did you feel safe there?" she asks.

"The spirit realm is hard to explain," I tell her.

"Was it beautiful?" Violet asks.

I don't know what Violet will see when she crosses over to the other side. She won't see my childhood room in Boston or meet Tilly, Cleo, and Dawn in their feathered hats and satin gowns. There won't be a desert or a sea. But whatever greets Violet in the afterlife will fit her image of beauty.

"What I saw may be different from what you see," I tell her. "But yes, the spirit realm is very beautiful."

My answer makes the ghost's face twist with regret. "It's . . . it's time for me to go outside too."

Miki rushes to Violet and grabs her hands. "No, not yet."

I now realize Caleb has completed his unfinished business. Maybe the same is true for Violet, and her reason to remain on this physical plane has also vanished.

"Please, Miki," Violet whispers.

Miki lets out a heartbreaking sob as Violet leaves the den and heads for the front door. Alexa rises from the sofa and consoles Miki. After weeping on Alexa's shoulder for a few moments, Miki lets Alexa gently guide her out of the house.

"How do you feel, Wednesday?" Danni-Lynn asks. "Do you think you can come outside with us?"

I put my feet on the floor. My head feels clear, and the pain in my chest is completely gone.

"Yeah, I can do it," I tell her.

When we get out on the porch, Miki, Violet, and Alexa are already standing down by the gate. But just as Danni-Lynn and I join them, Lincoln pulls up to the curb in his car.

"Okay, y'all, act normal," Alexa tells everyone. "Everybody looks fine. Even you, Wednesday."

When Olivia gets out of the car, she looks at us strangely, and I wonder if she can tell I've been possessed by a wicked ghost.

"We were just out here talking," I quickly say.

She studies each of us, but when she looks at Violet, the expression on her face changes from curiosity to recognition. Although she lost her gift many years ago, she's still a believer, and being this close to Violet, Olivia can feel the ghost's cold presence.

"Hey!" Jasmine leans out the passenger seat of Lincoln's car. "Did y'all get any good candy?"

"We did!" Danni-Lynn says too loudly and too cheerfully. "Only the best in this neighborhood!"

Jasmine waves at us, and Lincoln blows the horn before he drives away. Olivia returns her gaze to me, which makes my stomach gurgle with nerves.

"I'm going to let you talk to your friends a little bit

longer, Wednesday." She looks at the other girls, but her stare lingers again on Violet. "But y'all need to get home soon, okay? It's getting late."

We all mumble in agreement. Satisfied with our responses, Olivia walks to the porch and then goes inside the house.

Across the street, the Leehans are watching TV, and the blue light glows from the window.

Violet stares at the house and then slowly turns to us with sad eyes. "My parents don't live there anymore, so it isn't my home now. It hasn't been for a long time."

Miki dashes to Violet's side. "You could come stay with me. Right, Wednesday? I know I won't be able to see Violet after tonight, but next Halloween—"

"Miki," I interrupt her. "She can't stay with you."

"That's not fair!" Miki lets out a teary protest. "Just because she doesn't want to go back to her house doesn't mean she has to *leave*. Why can't you help her?"

"Wednesday can't do anything about that," Alexa says. "Violet doesn't have her family—"

"She has *me*!" Miki shrieks. "She has all of us! Isn't that enough?"

When Miki starts crying again, Danni-Lynn quickly embraces her. "Of course she has us, Miki."

Violet watches them with torn emotions. I walk toward her and slowly reach out for her hand. When she lets me take it, the cold pricks my skin.

"The longing to leave won't go away," I tell her.

"That's what Caleb told me," Violet says. "Even though I don't want to stay, it's still hard to leave."

"Goodbyes are always hard, but at least you can say it. So many people don't get that opportunity after they die."

"I . . . I'm glad you'll be there for them when I'm gone."

Violet goes to Danni-Lynn and Miki, and they open their arms to welcome her. Alexa follows and joins them in their group hug.

I witness this last connection as Violet says goodbye to each girl. Danni-Lynn laughs through her tears as they hold hands. Alexa tells Violet how much she'll miss her. Miki is too emotional, so Violet does the talking. They lean against each other, foreheads touching.

When she breaks away from her friends, she gives one last look at her house and then comes to me. After giving me a long, strong hug, she looks down Noble Avenue toward the park.

Caleb has appeared under a lamppost and smiles wide at us. But instead of wearing pajamas, he's dressed in short sleeves and pleated shorts. No dark bruise appears around his neck—the ghost's skin is sun-kissed and healthy. He's moved on from the horrible night of his death.

"I think I know where to go now," Violet tells me.

"I think so too," I say. "Goodbye, Violet."

I join the other girls in the street as the ghosts meet under the lamppost. When they begin their journey toward the park and their forms start to fade, Miki takes off and bolts down Noble Avenue. Alexa tries to run after her, but Danni-Lynn grabs Alexa's arm.

"Let her go," Danni-Lynn whispers.

"Violet!" Miki yells as she sprints down the street. "Violet, wait!"

When the ghost turns around, Miki stumbles to a stop and sways, putting her hands on her knees. The girls stare at each other in the distance.

"Don't worry about me, Violet!" Miki shouts. "I'll be okay!"

Violet smiles and gives a final wave. A few moments later, the ghosts disappear into the shadows of the park.

Miki trudges back to us, head hanging low and eyes filling with tears. "I *am* going to be okay. Right?"

Danni-Lynn pulls her into a hug. "You're going to be more than okay, Miki."

Alexa joins them and they form another tight circle. Again, I move away and don't insert myself, because I'm only a witness. But it doesn't stop the yearning to want what they have—a friendship with a mix of good and bad memories—what I've never had.

When Miki looks up and finds me standing alone by the curb, she opens the circle, offering a place for me.

"Come on, Wednesday," she says.

I slowly move forward until Danni-Lynn grabs me and giggles. The girls pull me into their tight hug and murmur their thanks to me.

"We're all going to be okay," I whisper.

CHAPTER THIRTY-THREE

The strong wind is brisk outside as I close the door to Nana's house. I button my coat and pull my hat over my braids before I rush down to the gate.

A few Halloween pumpkins sit on porches, but the skeletons and scarecrows are gone. Now holiday tree lights peek through some of the neighbors' windows.

Miki's latest club invitation is different—a sky-blue envelope with shimmering gold letters. When I arrive in her backyard, balloons with the same colors are fastened with ribbons to the small lamppost. Miki loves to stay on a theme.

I knock on the clubhouse door, and Miki gives me a tight hug before she pulls me inside.

"Wednesday, I've missed you!" she gushes.

I roll my eyes. "You talked to me on the phone an hour ago."

Danni-Lynn waves from the sofa. "Hey, Wednesday."

Two Beloved Bakery boxes are on the table with a pitcher of red punch and Miki's double-chocolate chip cookies.

"I'm surprised we decided to have a club meeting

during Thanksgiving break," I tell them. "I don't have much to report on my end, since I can't talk to the school ghosts—" Miki and Danni-Lynn burst out laughing, and it confuses me. "What's so funny?"

"You look so cute when you don't know what's going on," Danni-Lynn says. "Bless your heart."

"We're not here to talk about ghosts," Miki says.

There's another knock at the door, and Alexa comes in and hugs everyone before she sits next to Danni-Lynn on the sofa. I sink into the beanbag chair, and Miki clears her throat to get everyone's attention.

"I'm glad everyone accepted my invitation," she says. "In our officer meeting, Danni-Lynn and I decided we should expand beyond the club's original purpose. No offense, Wednesday."

"That's okay," I say. "I can be more than a medium."

Alexa shrugs. "Let's broaden our horizons. What did y'all have in mind?"

"Most clubs tend to focus on one thing, but we're not most clubs. *Obviously*," Miki says. "However, it could be good for us to do other things besides communicating with the dead."

"Exactly," Danni-Lynn chimes in. "One thing we can do as an official club is binge-watch the new season of *Loveburned* when it comes out in February."

"Ugh, it's the final one, right?" Miki sighs. "I don't think Leo Stacks will come back for another season."

"The volleyball team made it to regionals," Alexa offers. "Y'all can come to the game next week."

"Ah, congratulations!" Miki beams. "Yes, we can attend as an official club and come root for you."

"Olivia is having an art show during the holidays," I say, pride overflowing in my voice. "We can go to her opening."

"Wonderful idea!" Danni-Lynn says. "Your mama is *so* talented."

We discuss other things we could possibly do as an official club—things that don't involve the dead at all.

"Since we all agree on this idea, I motion that we move forward with a new name," Miki says. "But I think we should keep the original initials."

"I second this motion," Alexa says.

Danni-Lynn straightens up on the sofa. "We should call ourselves the Damsels Club."

"No." Miki frowns. "We're not going to be damsels."

"Do we have to keep the same initials?" I ask.

"We should do it in honor of Violet," Miki says.

Danni-Lynn opens the club notebook. "Time to brainstorm!"

"What about the Distinctive Comrades?" I say.

Miki shakes her head. "Seriously, Wednesday? Let's keep 'club' in our name at least."

Danni-Lynn writes in the club notebook and then grins in delight. "What about the Diva Club?"

Alexa takes the pen out of Danni-Lynn's hand. "You can't come up with any more names."

"We don't have a lot of choices," I say.

"What about the Diamond Club?" Alexa suggests. "Diamonds are my birthstone."

Miki searches the bookshelves and pulls out a thick book. She flips the pages of what I now see is a dictionary.

"I can't find any good candidates in here either." She plops on the sofa between Alexa and Danni-Lynn. "The Dead Club *is* a good name."

We all look at each other and come to a silent agreement, but Miki still makes us vote. After Danni-Lynn records the results, Miki pours a cup of punch for each of us.

"Let's do a toast!" she shouts. "To the Dead Club!"

We tap our cups together and then burst into silly giggles. The club will keep its name in our friend's honor. Although I didn't know Violet in life, I found out who she was in death—a brave ghost who fulfilled her purpose and crossed over to the other side.

I don't know if I'll become one of my family's strongest descendants, but I'll keep learning how to use my Lodestar so I can go talk to Nana and other ghosts in the spirit realm. Maybe one day I'll see Violet and Caleb again.

For so long, I've been lonely and afraid. I thought I had to hide my gift and ignore the dead until I met Miki, Danni-Lynn, and Alexa.

A secret club brought us together, and now I have the friends that I've always wanted.

ACKNOWLEDGMENTS

I've always wanted to write a novel about friendship. Unlike Wednesday, I didn't banish a wicked ghost or travel to the spirit realm, but I do have vivid memories of making friends in seventh grade at a new school.

I want to give thanks to my agent, Patrice Caldwell, for always being my steadfast advocate and to my editor, Kendra Levin, for guiding me to find the true heart of this story. I'm also very thankful for Kate Sullivan, Trinica Sampson-Vera, Joanna Volpe, and everyone at New Leaf Literary & Media.

Thanks to art director Lucy Ruth Cummins and artist Vivienne To for creating such a wonderful cover, and to Hilary Zarycky for the beautiful interior design.

So much appreciation to copy editor Megan Gendell and proofreader Ariel So for their expertise. Special thanks to Jan Mitsuko Cash for helping me with Miki's Japanese.

Thanks to Amy Beaudoin, Nicole Benevento, Amanda Brenner, Justin Chanda, Antonella Colon, Nicole Ellul, Alma Gomez Martinez, Victor Iannone, Michelle Leo, Lisa Moraleda, Tara Shanahan, and everyone on the Simon & Schuster team for helping me bring this book into the world.

While writing this novel, I found so much joy and solace in fandoms such as Star Wars, *Avatar: The Last Airbender*, *Star Trek: Discovery*, The Legendborn Cycle, and *Heartstopper*. I'm so grateful for the fan fiction, fan art,

ACKNOWLEDGMENTS

and overall love of these universes. I'm happy that I could showcase this kind of passion in Danni-Lynn. The book nerd in me is also happy to pay homage to *Wait Till Helen Comes* and Mary Downing Hahn.

As always, all the gratitude to the readers, booksellers, librarians, and educators who have supported me over the years. Y'all are my favorite people, and I wrote this book for you.

ABOUT THE AUTHOR

Karen Strong is the author of the critically acclaimed middle-grade novels *Just South of Home* and *Eden's Everdark*. She is also a Star Wars contributor featured in *Stories of Jedi and Sith* and the editor of the young adult anthology *Cool. Awkward. Black.* Born and raised in rural Georgia, Karen is an avid lover of strong coffee, yellow flowers, and night skies. You can visit her online at Karen-Strong.com.